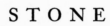

STONE

* STONE

a Novel by

Douglass Wallop

W · W · NORTON & COMPANY · INC ·
NEW YORK

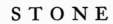
STONE

∗ one

Jeff Stone polished the glass, holding it up to the light, looking for smudges, and then, as he began to polish it again it broke in his hand. He shrugged, picked up the pieces and dropped them into the trash can.

It was 1941, the year that ended with the Japanese attack on Pearl Harbor, and Stone was spending the summer at the beach, working below sea level in a hotel taproom. He had just graduated from college and was waiting to be called into the army.

Stone was barely twenty-two years old, tall and rangy with hard shoulders and dark hair which had been cut very short for his graduation but which had not been cut since, so that it had become a soft brush on top and very shaggy on the back of his neck. His eyes were a very deep blue and his face was bony, a little lopsided and already heavily tanned. Every day he wore white ducks, of which he had two pair, and a dark blue sports shirt, of which he had three. Until this summer Stone had never worked in a taproom. He neither liked his job nor disliked it but it seemed as good a way as any to pass the time while waiting to be called into the army.

It was now the last week of June and Hitler had just invaded Russia, an act of aggression which had produced a very confused reaction in the United States since Germany was a villain-nation and Russia, at least until now, was also a villain-nation. There were some who claimed the invasion would help the Allied cause by siphoning off German strength and hence should be viewed with joy, but many others felt the United States should not help a communist country, nor even so much as root for one. There were some, Stone's father among them, who felt the invasion made U.S. entry into the war less likely, although there were many who felt the opposite.

Stone didn't know what to think. He felt that it was all beyond his control so he did his bartending job, waited to be called into the army, and tried not to brood about his family, which he knew was in grave danger of breaking up.

A great deal of his brooding was done in the taproom, particularly when he was working the afternoon shift. In the afternoon there was seldom much business because people were out on the beach getting sunburned and swimming in the ocean. Often in the afternoon he had the taproom to himself for hours at a time, although he could usually count on Shirley to drop by and pick at him. Shirley had a job upstairs in the hotel, room-clerking and typing letters. When she was off-duty she either went out on the beach to get more sunburn or else dropped by and picked at him to go to bed with her.

Early in the summer, in fact on the very night of his arrival, Stone had picked Shirley up on the boardwalk and taken her far up the beach. Although she herself was eager to the point of frenzy, he didn't feel like making love to her, and he couldn't be sure why. It didn't seem to make much sense because she was undeniably attractive, particularly her body. Yet because he felt it was expected of him, and because he expected it of himself, he began to nuzzle and maul her here and about, causing her to squirm and twitch, moan and groan and speak of beauty, etc., urging him to get on with it while the time was at hand, whereupon, in spite of his strange mood, he pulled himself together and did so, deliberately and even rather methodically driving himself home with long telling thrusts that made him think of low hard tennis shots or low line drives just over the infield, keeping it going, conserving himself, at which he was quite good for his age, until finally, against the crash of the ocean, Shirley let out a wail. Not until then did Stone let it all go and afterward found he was clutching dry sand in both hands and staring sadly through the darkness at the pencil lines of white foam that someone was writing on the dark face of the ocean at midnight.

"Oh, God . . ." Shirley said.

"That was great," Stone replied and then, feeling it had a desultory sound, he added politely, "really great"—yet he was disheartened and puzzled to realize how little he had felt, and how mechanical had been his performance. Sprawled face-down in the sand, still panting a little, he decided it must have something to do with the melancholy he felt about his family.

A few minutes later, as they lay in the soft sand looking up at the stars, Shirley made him feel even worse, telling him about her husband and her father hitting her, bludgeoning her with their fists, which was something Stone didn't want to hear about. It pained him to hear about it. Even though he had just met Shirley, barely knew her, he felt he wanted to jump up from the sand and go find her father and her husband and smash their heads against a brick wall. This, he knew, was impossible, yet at that moment it was what he wanted to do. He kept thinking about it while Shirley told him about her three-year-old daughter, who was being taken care of for the summer by Shirley's mother, back in the Pennsylvania coal mining country.

Stone had come to the beach to get away from the unpleasant family situation at home, which he was taking very hard, and because he didn't know what else to do with himself while he was waiting to be drafted. Whatever else the summer might bring, he decided then and there that Shirley would be a good person to stay away from, partly because he hadn't really enjoyed making love to her and partly because he had found it so disturbing, so deeply saddening, when she told him about being hit in the face by her father and husband. So far as he was concerned, it was strictly a one-night stand.

In expecting it to be no more than a one-night stand he felt he had been fully justified because that night, as they walked up the beach in the dark and sped through the getting-acquainted process, she told him that she was working as a waitress in a beer joint far down the boardwalk, at the very south end, miles away from where Stone worked, and that night it was quite true. She was.

But a couple of days later, to his surprise and hardly to his delight, she came into the taproom in a shiny black bathing suit without straps, perched herself on a barstool and said, "Hi—guess what?"

"What?" Stone asked.

"You'll never guess."

"Okay. Tell me."

"I'm working here now."

"Working where now?"

"Here. Right here at this hotel. Upstairs in the office."

"No *kidding?*" Stone said.

"No kidding."

"Well I'll be damned," Stone said, denting his finger with his thumbnail. "Doing what?"

"Typing letters. Taking reservations. Renting rooms. You know."

"Well I'll be damned." Stone paused. "You mean—you type?"

"Yeah. I just found out yesterday there was an opening and so I came down and talked to Mr. What's-his-name, Mr. Perry, and he hired me. Isn't that good?"

"That's great," Stone said.

"What's wrong with your cheeks?"

"Nothing." He had been pumping them up with air so that they bulged.

"You got the mumps?"

"No." He looked at her, trying to decide how he felt about her now that he could see her in the daylight. She was really built, this much he could concede, although she certainly didn't have the greatest face in the world. Yet she had very nice long blonde hair. Her eyes were rather small but on the other hand he liked the smooth golden tan of her legs. He particularly liked the combination of honey-blonde and black bathing suit. "You like typing better than being a waitress?" he asked.

"I love to type."

Stone took his bar rag and scrubbed at the bar, which didn't particularly need scrubbing. "Hey!" she said.

Stone looked up. "Yeah?"

"Did anybody ever tell you that you're great in bed?"

This made Stone feel uncomfortable and he parried by pointing out that they had never, strictly speaking, been in bed, which he realized was not a very clever thing to say, but it was all he could think of.

Shirley explained that she meant it as a figure of speech and that moreover the dry sand, still warm from the sun, was a nicer bed than a bed.

Stone nodded, wondering what else he should say and deciding for the moment to say nothing. He wished to hell she had kept her waitress job down at the south end of the boardwalk.

"Well . . ." she said, slipping from the barstool and smoothing the bottom of her black bathing suit. "Will I be seeing you, Jeff?"

Stone smiled weakly. "I don't see very well how you can *help* seeing me," he said, "since we're both working at the same hotel."

The day after Germany invaded Russia she came down in her black bathing suit again and said, "Hi—did you hear about Germany invading Russia?"

"Yeah, I heard," Stone said. "You want a beer or what?"

Shirley hauled up the front of her bathing suit and it slid down again. "A coke," she said. "I have to work tonight." She had a crazy rotating schedule. Some days she was off in the morning, some days in the afternoon and some at night.

Stone gave her the coke and she told him he was crazy, that she couldn't figure him out. Stone, knowing what she meant, began to feel uncomfortable. He grabbed his bar rag and got to work, wishing he had not been raised to worry so much about hurting people's feelings.

"Hey! That thing stinks!" Shirley sniffed at her wrist where the bar rag had brushed it.

Stone noticed that she had very fragile wrists. "I'm sorry." He sniffed the rag. "You're right. It does."

"What's the matter with you, Stone?"

"I told you I was sorry. I didn't mean to touch you with the damn bar rag."

"That's not what I mean," she said, and Stone knew it was not what she meant. But he had introduced the subject of the bar rag anyway.

"So tell me," she said. "What the hell's the matter with you?"

From the way she talked, he might have thought she was older and sort of whorish, but he knew she wasn't. She was only twenty-one. She was like a little girl trying to act tough and sophisticated. He supposed this was the way girls were who came from the coal mines. He had never known any girls from the coal mines before. "I don't know," he replied. "Hell. Nothing."

"I think something must be," Shirley said. "What is it?"

"I'm not sure," he said. "I'll have to figure it out."

Shirley looked disgusted. She got up from the barstool and put a nickel in the juke box, playing Artie Shaw's recording of *Pyramid* because she had already determined that Stone liked it, and that he was very tired of Tommy Dorsey's *I'll Never Smile Again*, which almost everybody played, even though by now it was a year old.

"Have you figured it out yet?" she asked, sitting on the barstool again and hauling up her bathing suit.

"I'm working on it," Stone said.

"Well, let me know when you figure it out," she said.

"Okay, I will."

"Is it because you think I might get serious about you?"

Stone shrugged, not knowing what to reply.

"If that's what you think then forget it," she said. "How could I ever get serious about somebody as crazy as you are? The hell with you, Stone."

She slipped from the barstool and left.

The taproom was called the Utopia Bar and Grill, a name thought up by Mrs. Perry before she died, but there was very little grill about it. Stone and Charlie, his co-worker, hated making sandwiches and they discouraged people from eating. If somebody asked for a sandwich they would say they were out of bread, that they were still waiting for the bread man and didn't know what could be keeping the bastard.

Stone liked the drowsy peace of the taproom in the afternoons. He also liked the idea of the taproom being below sea level, and he liked the way the floor looked—dark and permanently damp. He wasn't sure whether it looked damp because of the sea air or because so many people came in with wet bathing suits that dripped all over the floor. Since the taproom was below sea level, the only windows were up near the ceiling, horizontal slits like small transoms, and since the hotel faced east, the sun never hit the taproom except in the

morning, when it was closed. By afternoon it was always nice
and dark.

Even though the relative quiet of the taproom tended to
make him brood, Stone liked working afternoons, but so did
Charlie, so on weekdays they worked alternate shifts. On
weekends they both had to be on duty together at all hours.
The reason Charlie liked the afternoons was because in the
afternoons Charlie had great freedom to operate. Charlie was
quite an operator. He operated back in the storeroom where
all the cases of beer were kept. Charlie would take girls back
there, lock the door and bang them on a barstool when things
were quiet enough. Mr. Perry left the taproom pretty much to
Stone and Charlie, coming down only at midnight to check
out the cash. He asked Charlie what the hell the barstool was
doing in the storeroom all the time and Charlie said he kept
it there because sometimes he had to stand on it to reach the
beer cases at the top of the stack. Charlie had blue-black wavy
hair, weak shifty eyes, a boyish grin and a deep cleft in his
chin. When he grinned there were dimples in his cheeks. He
also had a country-boy accent and he talked very fast, sometimes tripping over his own consonants. When Charlie told
Mr. Perry about keeping the barstool there so he could reach
the beer cases, Stone found it very funny. Charlie told it very
earnestly, stuttering a little and looking Mr. Perry straight
in the eye, even though it obviously pained him to do so.
Stone went off to his room laughing, and for a while he didn't
think about all the things he hated thinking about.

One thing he hated thinking about was going off to war,
because the fact was that he didn't want to kill anybody and
didn't want anybody to kill him. He was also very much
afraid that his father was going to leave his mother, which
would have been bad enough at any time but would be even
worse if it happened while Stone was off in the war, possibly
getting himself killed.

He knew his father had a mistress and he knew her name was Ellen, although beyond this he didn't really know very much. Sometimes at night, lying in the darkness and trying to figure out what to do about it, he would imagine himself going to bed with Ellen, whoever she might be, and in this way somehow breaking up her affair with his father. He thought of what it would be like. He would be expert, deft and detached. He would probably hate her, yet the hatred would give him greater drive and greater overall effectiveness. He had learned this from reading Ernest Hemingway.

He had learned other things from Hemingway. From a short story he had learned that nothing was nothing was nothing, for the short story had said as much—although considering Hemingway's fondness for lapsing into Spanish, what it might have said was that nada was nada was nada, he couldn't remember for certain.

Stone also had great fondness for James Thurber and rather enjoyed seeing himself as a Thurber character, yet he knew that really to be one he would have to be older and married to a rather exasperating wife. Even so he often could see the world as a Thurber world, full of absurdity and non sequitur, and this, he thought, was simply a more good-natured way of seeing it all as nada.

Stone had four heroes. Two of these were Hemingway and Thurber. A third was Jesus Christ, whose guts he admired and with whom he occasionally held conversations. The fourth was Lester Young, who played tenor saxophone in Count Basie's band.

Although Charlie was far from a hero, Stone sometimes envied him his prowess with girls. With Charlie's experience he felt he might have a chance of knocking off his father's mistress if he ever should find out who she was. But he did not envy Charlie's callousness. He could never be as amoral as Charlie and didn't want to be. If he had shared this trait with

Charlie he would not have felt the way he felt about Shirley, for as the days passed and she continued to seek him out he decided that taking her up the beach and making love to her had been a careless thing to do and he felt guilty about it. He supposed that what he mainly felt guilty about was that he hadn't really felt like doing it and certainly didn't feel like doing it again.

But when he was alone in his room at night, it was not of Shirley that he thought, nor of Charlie, nor even of Hemingway. It was of himself, somewhere in Germany, bayonet upraised, being asked, or asking himself to drive the blade into the soft flesh of someone he had no desire to kill. Then he would see himself dead on German soil, sprawled beneath some German tree, and then he would think of his home. It was empty. He walked into the dining room. Nobody was sitting at the dining room table, and he felt a sharp, devastating sensation of emptiness, of total sadness.

✳ two

Where Stone slept was a lousy place to sleep, a tiny room in the hotel basement, meaning that not only did he work below sea level but also slept below sea level. His room was like a cell, the only difference being that he could more or less come and go as he pleased; probably more of a dungeon than a cell because he had always thought of dungeons as darker than cells and it was very dark.

The basement was lined with passageways and it was easy to get lost. From the storeroom where the beer was kept a passageway led back to three rooms. The first was Charlie's room, the next was the so-called ladies room for the use of ladies who patronized the taproom, and the last was Stone's room. These rooms each had a window with a view of nothing at all. Stone didn't even try to look from his window because outside it was black, the reason being the long veranda that ran the entire length of the hotel on the street side. Stone's view was of the bricked-in darkness beneath the veranda and he kept his raincoat hanging over the window so he wouldn't forget and glance out, expecting to see something that wasn't there, such as a sunlit sidewalk or a glimpse of blue ocean.

It was such a terrible room that Stone at times found himself laughing about it, particularly when he considered that lodging represented part of his salary. At other times, when he was feeling sad, he found its gloominess appropriate and even its meagerness appealed to him. There was nothing in it except the cot on which he slept, and the window that looked out upon nothing, and the biggest damned pillar he had ever seen, right in the middle of the room and occupying a good half of the room's total cubic footage. The pillar was made of convex cement blocks, heavily whitewashed. Stone assumed it must be holding up half the weight of the hotel. There was also a crate, possibly an orange crate, which stood on end and served as a bureau. Inside on the makeshift shelf, the crate's divider, he kept his other shirts and his other pair of white ducks.

The room had only a screen door which had neither spring nor hook, so when he went to bed at night he placed his shoes against it to keep out the rats. He knew his shoes were not heavy enough to stop any very determined rat but he felt the rat would at least think twice.

Sometimes at night he would lie on his cot and wonder

what he should do about his family, holding a conversation now and then with Christ, Who so far had been ineffectual and even rather offhand.

On other nights Stone talked with William, the head bellman, who wanted to be a weather man. After passing Stone's screen door, the passageway was immediately blocked by a partition which divided the white help's quarters from the colored help's quarters, thus preventing members of either race from straying into the quarters of the other. William's room was the first on the other side of the partition and hence William and Stone, outposts of their respective races, had a common bedroom wall. Stone's cot was against the wall and so was William's, on the other side, and since the wall was made of some flimsy substance like beaver board Stone had found it an easy matter to jab a hole in the wall with the handle of his hairbrush, and he and William talked through the hole whenever they felt like it. William had a radio that he played all the time, including all night long, falling asleep with it still playing, and at first Stone had had to wake him up to turn off the radio, but now he was accustomed to it and could fall asleep with it on, although sometimes he listened to it. When William tuned in the Joe Louis-Billy Conn fight on June 18, Stone asked him to turn up the volume and they listened to the fight together. Stone realized that to have Louis, a black man, win the fight against Conn, a white man, was very important to William, and as the fight progressed he could tell from the way William was muttering on the other side of the wall that he was disappointed that Louis was not able to knock out Conn until the thirteenth round. When the fight ended, Stone said through the wall that Joe Louis was a tremendous champion, and William, happy now that the knockout was a fact, replied generously that Billy Conn must be a truly great boxer to last as long as he lasted.

Stone found it disgusting that there should be a partition

dividing white from black sleeping quarters. It was, however, part of the rigid system insisted upon by Mr. Perry, and he knew there was little that he personally could do about it. To compensate, he made bitter sarcastic remarks about the system, sometimes only to himself. He was also very nice to all the colored help and was in fact rather eagerly patronizing even though all he intended being was nice and compassionate and it was in this way that he thought of himself—not as patronizing. He was pleased that his room and William's had a common bedroom wall with a hole in it, feeling that in this colorful, offbeat way he and William had managed to defy the system. When William talked through the hole to Stone he was always free and easy and even rather breezy, yet when he and Stone happened to meet during the day around the hotel, William was shy and deferential and seemed embarrassed. William was slight of build and always looked clean and dapper in shiny black trousers and starched white bellman's jacket. When he saw Stone by day he would grin and look down at his small shiny black shoes. It was as though he preferred keeping the hole in the wall a secret line of communication. Stone, who from reading Hemingway was given to finding symbolism in certain situations, wondered if this meant the two races were only able to find true communication through a hole in a wall.

On the other side his room adjoined the ladies room and this Stone found distracting. For one thing the toilet was being flushed incessantly all through the evening. It was bad enough when someone was in there alone, but when two friends went in together it was much worse. They talked and flushed and laughed and flushed and talked and Stone could hear every word they said, which often had to do with stockings and how they hoped the government would not start rationing silk stockings the way it was already rationing gasoline. Sometimes the talk was coarse and this came as a surprise to

Stone, who had no sisters and whose mother was a complete lady. One night somebody came in singing a phrase or two of *East of the Sun, West of the Moon*, then broke off and said she wished that *she* were east of the sun with Clark Gable and that Clark Gable was snatching and tearing at her shirtwaist. They of course had no idea that anybody's bedroom was right next door. After midnight, when the taproom closed, the ladies room was quiet.

Shirley found out where Stone slept and came down and stood outside in the passageway, looking through the screen door. She said, "Hi—so *this* is where you sleep?"

Stone said it was and she said, "I just wanted to see where you slept." She then came in, sat on the edge of his cot and sighed.

Stone felt certain that she had nothing on under her pink gingham blouse, and since she was built as she was he could not help but find this attractive. Her long blonde hair looked as though it had just been washed because each strand seemed to be separated from all the others, all loose and clean and looking as if it were charged with electricity. Shirley had sleepy looking eyes. They drooped at the outer corners and her mouth also drooped and sometimes her face could look very tragic and mournful, but once again he realized that it was not, generally speaking, a pretty face. Her nose had a slight hook and her brow was a little too wide and yet somehow he still thought of her face as delicate and fragile and he could not figure out why, unless it was because he knew it was a face that had been hit many times by a man's fist. He hated thinking about it.

She was smiling at him and he looked at the way the light from his lamp was shining on her hair. He felt that if he placed his palm on her head and pushed down a little, her hair would spring right back up under his hand because of all the electricity in it.

"Do you mind?" she asked.

"Mind what?" Stone said.

"Mind if I sit here." She picked up the newspaper he had been reading. "Gosh," she said, "I'd like to see that, wouldn't you? Listen," she said, reading. " 'This picture provides at least a laugh a minute—' "

"Oh God," Stone said.

" 'There are no blushes mixed up with the laughs because the action is—*motivated* by—*impulses* that may be brisk and brash but at the same time are disarming and honest.' "

"I don't want to see it," Stone said. "What is it?"

"Listen. 'A fast-moving frolic in which an American flier, ferrying bombs to Britain, almost overnight woos and wins a beautiful young woman whom he meets in an otherwise deserted bomb shelter . . .' " Shirley let the newspaper fall to the floor. "*One Night in Lisbon*, starring Madeleine Carroll and Fred MacMurray."

"It sounds lousy," Stone said.

"What are *you*—a snob?"

"Hell no," Stone said. "I'm frankly about as far from being a snob as anybody you could ever find."

"Yeah, I'll bet. I'll bet you were sitting there thinking what a lousy reader I am."

"Like hell I was," Stone said.

She smiled as if she didn't believe him. "Listen, Stone, what have you figured out?"

"Figured out about what?"

"You were going to figure out why you don't find me attractive, remember?"

"Hell, Shirley, I *do* find you attractive."

"Well then . . ."

Stone looked at the floor.

"You stupid dumb bastard," Shirley said.

Stone grinned. "I don't know," he said. "It's just something . . . something inside me."

"What do you mean, something inside you?" Shirley began to smile. "What's inside you, Stone?"

"It's very hard to describe," he said.

Shirley still sat on the edge of the cot. She stared pensively at the filthy floor, with the lamp shining on her very clean hair. "Okay," she said finally. "But you *do* find me attractive though? You don't feel that just because I'm from the coal mines—"

"Oh, *hell*," Stone said. "Don't talk like that. Don't deny your roots".

"Okay, okay." Shirley frowned. "I guess it's mostly my own fault anyway. I don't feel very happy tonight."

"Why not?"

She sighed and said it was because she had had a letter from her mother that day and her mother had asked her what her plans were for the fall, and this had started her thinking. "I don't know what I'm going to be able to do for her," she said. "I'd like to give her advantages. But how in the hell am I going to do it, Stone?"

Stone knew that she meant her three-year-old daughter.

She talked for a long while about her daughter and her husband and her father and Stone lay on the cot with his eyes closed, not wanting to listen but listening. She was hitting him hard in another weak spot because he loved kids, especially little kids, and he wondered if she was doing it on purpose, the bitch. She was saying she thought that by the time her daughter grew up she'd probably have a good chance of marrying somebody who wouldn't hit her, and then said:

"I think the custom of hitting women is gradually dying out, don't you?"

Stone writhed and then deliberately banged the back of his head against the wall.

"What in the hell's the matter with you, Stone?" Shirley demanded. "What are you doing to yourself?"

"Nothing."

Shirley grinned. "My Uncle Hutch always told me that anybody who goes to college has to be crazy and I believe it."

She went on to say that her Uncle Hutch was local delegate to the United Mine Workers and once had had lunch with John L. Lewis.

"Well, anyway . . ." She got up from the cot and raised her arms high above her head and stretched. The pink gingham blouse stretched. "What do you have your shoes against the door for, Stone?"

Stone told her and she shuddered. "I'm not so sure I want to sleep here after all," she said.

Stone shrugged.

This made her angry. "You're crazy, Jeff. You really are *crazy*. The *hell* with you."

Angrily she stalked out. He heard her go into the ladies' room and slam the door. For a few seconds more he lay on the cot, feeling sorry for her, then he got up and went out into the corridor. "Hey . . . Shirley . . . are you in there?"

There was no reply.

"*Shirley* . . ."

"*What?*"

"Listen. . . . There's something I have to tell you. . . . It's not your fault. It's mine."

There was no reply. He heard the toilet being flushed and then the door swung open. She was frowning at him. "What are you talking about?"

"Come on back a minute."

He took her hand and drew her back into his room. They sat side by side on the edge of the cot. "Now listen," he said, "and I'll try to make you understand. It's not that I don't think you're attractive. You're plenty attractive. I'm the one. I'm sort of a mess."

Shirley was looking at her fingernails. "Why are you a mess?"

"I don't know. It's sort of like I've been—gored, you might say."

Shirley let her hand fall to the cot. She turned and stared at him. "You've been what?"

"Gored."

"You mean—*stuck?*"

He nodded. "Sort of."

"What stuck you, Stone?"

"Well . . ." Stone squirmed into a new position, so that he could rest his head against the wall. "Nothing in a physical sense," he said, "but the effect is the same as if I'd been gored —by a bull or something. So that I can't go to bed with you. What I mean is that I can't really go to bed with anybody that I really like. . . ." Stone frowned. It had seemed like a good idea when he started out but now he wasn't so sure.

"That you really *like?*"

"Or that I think highly of . . . do you see what I mean?"

"Jesus, Mary and Joseph!" Shirley shook her head with amazement. Her eyes danced. "Do you remember what I said a few minutes ago about my Uncle Hutch and what he thought of people who went to college? Well, boy! My Uncle Hutch—he sure as hell knew his onions!"

"All right, forget it," Stone said.

"Do you have any idea what you're talking about?" she demanded.

Stone wasn't at all sure that he did.

"Listen, Stone, no bull ever gored you, I know *that* for a fact—unless it happened just in the past three weeks."

"That's not the point," Stone said.

"Well what *is* the point then?"

"All right, let's just say that I've been psychically gored if you want to. Can you agree to that?"

"Agree to *what?*"

"That I've been gored in the psyche."

"I can agree to *one* thing and that is that you're really a crazy son of a bitch, Stone, no kidding, you really are."

"Okay," he said. "I'll try to explain it. Listen, did you ever read much of Ernest Hemingway?"

"No, I'm just a poor uneducated bitch, *you* know that."

"Okay, he wrote this book—no you're not either—and it's all about this poor guy who got all shot up in the war so that he can't go to bed with anybody."

"You mean physically?"

"Right."

"You mean he got shot in the joint?"

"Right. . . . Anyway, he and this English woman are in love with each other but it's very sad because they can't do anything about it."

Shirley's head now was resting against the wall next to his. She raised one leg, pointing her toe at the ceiling. Looking at her leg, she frowned with concern. "So what *do* they do about it?"

"Nothing. They just sort of sit around in Paris drinking, and then they go to bull fights."

Shirley's leg dropped. "That's all they do?"

"Pretty much."

"Is that what made you think of being stuck by a bull? Because they went to bull fights?"

"The bull fights have nothing to do with it. That's just one of the things they do with themselves. Anyway it's very sad and melancholy. It's a tragedy."

"And this guy is you?"

"Similar."

27

Shirley was smiling a sad smile. "That's a lot of crap, Stone." She looked into his eyes. "What you're really saying is that you don't think I'm attractive. Why not admit it?"

Stone shook his head. "That's not true," he said. "But here's something else. Who in the hell am I? I'm nothing. There are plenty of other guys down here who'd lay you at the drop of a hat. You can get laid all day long if you want to."

Shirley was still looking into his eyes. "Go to hell, Stone," she whispered and left, closing the screen door carefully behind her.

Stone lay there for a while, staring at the ceiling. Then he got up and propped his shoes against the screen door. Lying again in his cot, he tried to read. At midnight, when the noise ended in the ladies room, he turned off his light and lay there thinking of what he had told Shirley. She was right. What he had told her was a lot of crap. He could lay her if he wanted to. It would be very easy to have a summer fling with her, yet something held him back. He wondered if he might have felt differently if she had not told him about getting hit in the face. On the other hand the real reason was probably because he felt so sad about his family, and so depressed about the war. Anyway, it wasn't all that important. She'd find somebody.

After a while he heard William come in next door. William was going with Martha, the assistant pastry cook, but they both worked until late and so they didn't go any place to speak of except to bed. "Hey, man," William called cautiously, but Stone didn't feel like talking so he didn't answer, and heard William say in a low voice, "He'sleep," and then he heard Martha giggle and then the radio came on and Stone fell asleep listening to the music and the sound of William and Martha making good-natured love.

✳ three

The next morning Stone took a long walk northward, far beyond the last hotel. When the boardwalk ended, he jumped down to the sand and walked on and on, reaching the dunes where he had taken her the night they made love. He looked for what he thought might have been the exact spot, searching for the imprint of their bodies in the sand, idly wondering. Then, ankle-deep in the water, he looked out over the backlit emptiness of the ocean, feeling very close to Europe, feeling a sense of abeyance. Over there was the reality. He peered toward the horizon, feeling that if he listened very intently he might hear the sound of gunfire, the sound of British bombers droning their way back home after morning raids against Germany. Standing very still, he listened, and could hear only the lazy rhythm of the surf.

To the south, through the sun-drenched morning haze, he could see the tiny dots that he knew to be beach umbrellas. He started walking back again and as he drew closer the umbrellas grew larger and filled in with color. They were lined up near the water's edge in a long row and their shadows fell diagonally, in uniform puffs toward the northwest.

When he reached the boardwalk he climbed up again and then, glancing toward the beach, he saw a man in dark swimming trunks down near the water. For a brief moment he thought that it was his father. The man disappeared beneath one of the umbrellas and Stone hesitated, then walked on, wondering. The distance had been great, the glimpse brief. He knew that it could not have been his father because his father would not have come down to the beach without getting in touch with him.

In his room he found a message to call a long distance operator's number. His mother had called and when he saw the message he linked it with the man he had seen on the beach, but there was no link. His mother said she hadn't called for anything special, only to see how he was. She talked about his two younger brothers and about the new wallpaper she was planning to get for the living room, and she told him to enjoy his summer because who could tell where he might be the following summer, which would be the summer of 1942 —although, she went on hopefully, if the United States did not actually enter the war, and there were quite a few of her bridge girls who thought it would not, then maybe he wouldn't even be drafted. His mother's voice was cheerful, the young voice of a young mother, and in his mind's eye he could see her smiling into the phone, standing before the kitchen window.

Stone asked about his father and she said his father had been working very hard and that he felt the heat more than she did and more than his brothers did, particularly since his brothers were spending every day in the public swimming pool.

From this conversation Stone concluded that his mother still did not know about his father's mistress.

She knew, of course, that his father was sleeping up on the third floor, but perhaps this was all she did know, that his father was sleeping up in Stone's old room, surrounded by pictures left over from Stone's boyhood, autographed pictures of Joe Cronin, Goose Goslin and Heinie Manush.

That's the way it had all started, with his father moving from the four-poster, canopied bed they had shared for so long and sleeping instead on the hard, narrow studio couch upstairs on the third floor.

In early spring Stone had gone down to his father's office

and they talked about it. To Stone the talk was a nightmare and the discovery of a new world. Until then he had felt the world was a well-ordered place but the talk and what came afterward left him with a tilted feeling of imbalance.

His father told him that sleeping upstairs was a matter of principle and of manly integrity, and that in any case it was all just a temporary disagreement having to do with attitudes.

Stone sat in a straight chair, next to his father's desk, and his father sat in the swivel chair behind the desk, swiveling. On his father's desk there were pictures of Stone and his two brothers, but none of his mother. Stone looked at the fingerprints that smudged the glass top of the desk while his father explained about the gravy boat and Stone said that in his opinion the gravy boat was a small matter, certainly not important enough to disrupt a marriage, and his father agreed that it was a small thing but symptomatic. Stone said he didn't even remember any trouble about a gravy boat, whereupon his father explained that more than once the gravy boat had slid in its unattached dish, spilling gravy either on his plate or the tablecloth or both, and once even in his lap. He said that if he had asked Stone's mother once to buy a gravy boat with plate attached he had asked her a hundred times, all to no avail, and that it was symptomatic of her disregard for him as a husband and as a *man* that she had never seen fit to honor his wishes regarding the gravy boat. If she had bought one with plate attached, then it would have been impossible for the gravy boat to slip and slide about, and the marriage hence would have been on a better footing.

Stone realized that what his father was saying about the gravy boat might have been funny, except that his father did not consider it funny and Stone could not laugh. He could only feel the sense of living for the first time in an idiot-world. He asked his father whether everything would be okay if his mother now bought a gravy boat with plate attached, and his father said it would not mean as much now as it would have meant if she had bought it before he moved up to the third floor, explaining that if she bought it now it would mean she was only doing so under duress.

"My God!" Stone said.

"You can 'my God' all you want to," his father said, "but when you get older, Jeff, you'll understand."

Stone could not really believe that what had come between his mother and father was a gravy boat. Even so, three days later he went downtown again after his last class to buy a gravy boat with plate attached. While a salesgirl stood by, he deliberated between one of pale blue and one with rosebuds looping around the top edge, finally choosing the one with rosebuds. Carrying the package up to his father's office, he felt rather good about it. The one he had picked out wasn't bad looking at all. He presented the package and as his father opened it, Stone watched his face. His father said "Thanks, Jeff," in a husky voice and then cleared his throat hard, recovering quickly. "Thanks," he said again, this time in a ringing, controlled voice. "This is something we could have sure used a long long time ago." But Stone saw his jaw harden and his eyes grow clear, and he knew that what his father was saying was that it was too late.

A week or so later, when there was gravy, the new gravy boat appeared on the table. His father used it grudgingly.

Stone lived at home his senior year, dayhopping to class, and one morning in early May after his father had gone to the office he happened to wear his father's bathrobe to breakfast because his own was at the cleaner's. While he was eating breakfast he became aware of a wad of paper in one of the pockets. He took it out, saw that it was a note on pale blue paper and quickly put it back again because his mother was in the kitchen. A few minutes later, when she went out to the store, he spread the note on the dining room table and read it.

It began, "O my darling," and went on to rhapsodize at great length about the virtues of his father and then talked of counting the months until they no longer would have to sneak about. It was signed, "All my love, Ellen."

Feeling very hot and itchy in the scalp, Stone folded the note and stuffed it back into the pocket of the bathrobe. He sat staring into his empty plate and then at the wall, listening to the silence, the faint whizzing sound of total silence.

After that he found it hard to look his father in the eye and hard to talk to him. His father, for his part, seemed to find it hard to talk to Stone. He seemed sad and puzzled, but more defiant than regretful, as if he felt that Stone's remoteness was merely the outgrowth of their talk about the gravy boat. When he did talk to Stone it was often to say that he shouldn't let anything bother him, that he should just concentrate on getting good grades and graduating so that he would have his college degree before he went into the service. Once he asked Stone a question he had sometimes asked in the past, "Well, who do you think is the better hitter, Ted Williams or Joe DiMaggio?" It was as if his father were asking him to remember the two of them, son and father, side by side at the ball park on so many afternoons in so many summers, sitting in the upper deck where they always sat, high above the third base line, looking down upon the shadowed infield and the sunny green brilliance of the outfield; father and son in close companionship and harmony.

Stone knew the world was filled with broken homes, yet he had always felt that his own home and family were special, and it had always seemed to him that his mother and father were very close. He could see his father in the twilight of a winter's day, pulling up to the curb in a 1931 Ford with the spare tire mounted on the back; and his mother, leaving the kitchen where she had been cooking supper, moving quickly to the front door to greet him, to thank him, it seemed, perhaps for so cheerfully and eagerly expending his youth in the service of three sons. Smiling, she opened the door for him and in the orange cone of light from the ceiling fixture she stood waiting, a young slender mother with auburn hair and a quick, joyful laugh. If it had been a home of anger, despair, cruelty—but it had not. In his eyes it was the happiest of homes, the best of families.

As the spring days passed, Stone felt his responsibility keenly, yet even more keenly he felt his helplessness. Knowing his father's secret was a burden he did not want. He felt he could not tell his father about reading the note, nor could he tell his mother about Ellen. He didn't know what to do.

Graduation was lousy and even though he won second honors he felt heartsick, and then even worse after it was over to see the way his mother, in her new pale green dress, linked her arm through his father's arm as they threaded their way through the crowd, moving toward the rear of the gymnasium where Stone stood in his cap and gown. The glimpse of them together struck him painfully and he supposed it was because in his mother's face there was hope and innocence while in his father's face there was something sheepish, and something false. So he turned his back when he saw them coming and bent to a drinking fountain, sipping a little and then taking off his cap and letting the stream of water play over his face, thinking of the way his mother had linked her arm through his father's. "Congratulations, Jeff," his father said. Stone turned. His mother kissed him. Her smile was joyful. His father shook his hand hard and then embraced him, saying again, "*Congratulations, Jeff,*" and Stone knew that in a way his father was congratulating himself because he had been able to afford to send a son to college after almost two decades of no money, but he also knew from the light in his father's eyes that his father loved him and that he felt deeply guilty. His mother said, "We're so proud of you, honey. I had no idea you were graduating with honors, you said you weren't doing so well this semester." Stone nodded, smiled, then had to turn away again, for in spite of all he could do to control himself there were tears in his eyes. His mother smiled at him, knowing that tears were appropriate to graduations. His father looked at him sadly and moved to the water fountain, glancing back over his shoulder just before he bent to drink.

For a couple of days Stone hung around home, feeling the hollowness, feeling the burden of his secret. What he felt was beginning to show, and on the second day his mother asked him if something was wrong. He said no, he was okay. Putting on her broad-brimmed green gardening hat, she went out into the back yard, down by the white picket fence and worked in her flower beds. Watching from the kitchen window, he frowned. There was something just in the way she loosened the dirt and pulled out the weeds that made him think she might know. He decided he was imagining it, but even so it seemed better if he got out. Whatever he did around home would only make matters worse. Feeling as he felt, he might somehow betray what he knew about Ellen and propel a crisis that might not come.

Not knowing what else to do, he got a ride to the beach and found the job in the taproom.

Stone until now had been out on the beach infrequently, achieving a light coating of tan which he felt was enough for protection but which, as it turned out, was not.

In the afternoon, after thinking he had seen his father duck behind an umbrella and after telephoning his mother, he put on his trunks and lay on the beach in front of the hotel, closing his eyes against the blazing sun. He felt deeply depressed. His life was lousy and he felt powerless to do anything about it. Yet mingled with the feeling of depression was anger that he should be reduced to such a state of paralysis, that he should feel so immobilized, and he hardly knew which to blame more—himself or the fates which had brought it all to pass. With his hands at his sides, he gripped sand in both fists, unable to keep it from trickling swiftly away no matter how hard he squeezed.

Although he had not intended to, Stone fell asleep where he lay. It was after five when he awoke and the life guards were going off duty. Within an hour his reddened flesh hurt like hell and by nine o'clock that evening he was on fire. He took off all his clothes and paced up and down in his dungeon, swearing and moaning, then he went around and took a shower but when he got back to his room it was worse again, so he went back to the shower and stayed there until Mr. Perry came thumping down to the bathhouse wanting to know who was using the shower at that time of night, wasting water and electricity and whatnot. He told Stone he should have had sense enough not to stay out in the sun so long, that this was where the trouble lay, which was exactly what Stone had been thinking. He then asked if Stone had tried Noxzema or Johnson's Baby Powder. Stone said no, and Mr. Perry went upstairs and came back with some Noxzema, which Stone took back to his room and rubbed all over himself. He then tried to go to sleep, but in about five minutes he leapt up and drove his fist through the ceiling which, like the wall, was very flimsy.

About midnight he heard William come in and he told William about it. William said he shouldn't have stayed out on the beach in the sun so long, which was just what Mr. Perry had said and exactly what Stone himself had been thinking.

36

His pain was so great that the fatuousness of William's well-intended remark made him hysterical and William, hearing him laugh and thinking he must be feeling better, said smugly, "Trouble is you got *started* too late, man. About five thousand *years* too late. Ha ha ha." At this Stone put his fist through the ceiling again and flopped in his cot and tried to imagine that it was somebody else's pain and that he was just lying there, witnessing it. The trouble was that it made him think of his father and his father's mistress, and he lay there for hours, thinking about them in searing streaks and patches of burnt skin.

Toward three in the morning he got up from his cot, carried his flaming body out to the beach and dumped it into the ocean, lying face down just offshore, rising and falling with the waves but looking up now and then at the dimly-lit lobby of the hotel, measuring distance to make sure he was not being washed out to sea in the dark of night. The thought terrified him and for a while he examined his own terror. He began to tread water, looking eastward toward Europe, where the killing was. Then he floated face-down again, wondering if William truly had once been white, five thousand years ago, before the deep burn began. And he thought of Joe DiMaggio breaking the record for hitting safely in consecutive games, which Joe DiMaggio had done just that very week and which he was still doing, chalking up each day a new record of his own. He had broken the old record on the very same day that Jan Ignace Paderewski died. Meanwhile a giant, closely-contested tank battle waged on the Eastern Front. The Russians were putting up fierce opposition, puzzling Hitler, while somewhere his father and Ellen copulated and calculated, puzzling Stone.

When he came out of the ocean, he ran swiftly to his room, wanting to lie down on his cot while his body was still wet. But it dried quickly and as it dried the skin was drawn tight over the bones of his shoulders, pricking a million nerve ends. Possessed by pain, he jumped up from his cot and, naked by the huge pillar, performed a clog dance in the dark, croaking out nonsense lyrics renouncing his parents, damning their marital troubles, feeling a fierce, savage self-pity.

Out of breath, hoarsely panting, he flung himself again upon his cot. As the panting subsided, the pain of the sunburn increased, and now flickering images began to fall upon his brain with the speed of light, like the fall and flow of shuffled cards . . . a glimpse of his mother's hands clasped tight, of his father's face, of rain falling on cobblestones, a bloody bayonet, a malevolent smile.

The pain of the sunburn merged with the aching pain of his spirit and the two seemed to become one.

He lay motionless upon the damp sheets, forcing his body to remain still, but even as he did so his brain seemed to slip out of control, jerking through the darkness in bright, jagged streaks, a lunatic brain lashing him with questions about the reality of pain, of pleasure, of all human feeling.

He heard the questions and writhed, for as he examined them they disturbed him deeply, so infinite were the possibilities, so blurred and bottomless the depths.

Spreadeagled in the darkness, he stared into chaos, questioning for the first time in his life the fragile, flimsy makeshift fabric that always had given meaning to non-meaning.

As he lay in torment under the brain's inquisition, the pain of the sunburn seemed to fade, although he knew that it still must be there because his flesh was still on fire, drawn tight over the hard bones of his shoulders.

Yet by thinking upon it, examining it, he had somehow diminished it, momentarily reduced it to a word. But to say that pain was unreal and only a word was to feel panic and now he welcomed back the pain that he had sought to expel, feeling a crazed relief as the searing of his flesh registered as pain.

For pain was more than a word, it was real, and to think otherwise would be to cross over the line into insanity, or to become a piece of machinery to which there was no good no evil, no right, no wrong.

To a piece of machinery the majestic peak of a mountain would have no more beauty than a dungheap, the quiet waters of a lagoon no more beauty than a pool of fresh blood.

And why, he asked himself, should they?

To a piece of machinery the stricken face of a child, a brother, a mother, would mean no more, no less, than the face of one smiling with joy. Flesh whole would have no more meaning than flesh gouged by a bayonet.

And why, he asked himself, should they?

He could find no logic, no words, with which to give answer. He could say that the answer had a mighty pulse-beat, the sound of thunder, the depth of time. He could say that the answer reverberated all through his being, music without words.

But the answer remained elusive—as elusive as music, as elusive as time.

To a piece of machinery, no course was better than its opposite, and this would be invaluable in time of war, invaluable to one about to drive a bayonet into the neck of another.

A piece of machinery could not be hurt by things that were hurtful. Unhurt, it would merely stop functioning.

Throughout the long night he lived in a shadow world he had never known, tantalized, brutalized by his own brain.

Although no daylight penetrated to his dungeon room, when he turned on the lamp and took his watch from the orange crate he saw that it was nearly six-thirty.

With the lamp on, he lay staring at the ceiling, feeling at last a sense of calm. In the end, the fantastic pain of the sunburn had acted to cauterize. The tissue of shock, the tissue of fear, had been seared white and hard.

It was a world where grown men hit girls in the face, a world dedicated to mass killing of those who wanted to live on, a world in which the relationships of a lifetime could be destroyed by a cool bitch named Ellen.

The hell with it. He was not the first person to face a broken home, to face death in war, nor would he be the last. It was a ridiculous, absurd world, and he would cultivate absurdity. Numbly, or perhaps jauntily, depending upon his mood, he would accept the world as one in which cause had come unhinged from effect, and when things got too much for him he would stare into space of perhaps do a clog dance.

✳ four

And so in the days that followed, Stone came out of his room, looking about him with a cold eye, determined to be untouched, regarding the people about him as objects of mild curiosity, people who day by day would prove his conviction that it was all nothing, all absurd, the people with whom he would live in these last days before he would go off to kill and be killed.

There was Charlie and he could look at Charlie and feel nothing, neither disliking him nor liking him. He could begin to realize, and care not at all, that Charlie was probably a crook, for the cash had begun to come up short, just a little, never more than a few dollars and many nights not at all.

There was Mr. Perry, an angry tense man in tan pongee, who told people he had wept the summer before, when the Germans took Paris, but who now seemed oblivious of the war, oblivious of anything that went on beyond his hotel.

Each night, just at midnight, Mr. Perry came down to the taproom with a small blue denim sack, checked the cash register, counted the money, dumped it into the sack, and then counted the beer, for it was the beer count that told the tale. One night the beer was eight bottles short, once twelve and finally nineteen short. On the night it was nineteen bottles short, Mr. Perry said, "Boys, I own this hotel lock-stock-and-barrel, and this has got to stop." Stone looked into Mr. Perry's pale blue eyes and nodded. Charlie said quickly, "I broke a couple bottles today, you break any bottles, Stone?" Stone said yes, he had broken a couple of bottles, although he hadn't. "I spilled one on a lady, went all down the front of her," Charlie went on earnestly. "So I give her another one to replace it with."

Stone decided that Charlie must be lifting a few dollars now and then but he didn't care. It seemed unimportant.

Charlie told Stone that after quitting college he had held a number of jobs and of them all he liked working in the taproom best. He said he liked taking girls back to the storeroom and he liked it even when he wasn't taking girls back to the storeroom. He just liked being there. One day he told Stone his philosophy of taprooms. He said that what a taproom looked like didn't matter, the main thing was a friendly atmosphere, just so nobody wanted any sandwiches, and that a barstool moreover was a perfect height.

Stone speculated on Charlie's reaction if he were to find that his father was a liar and a phoney. He decided that

Charlie would not give a damn and that if he did give a damn he'd simply make more trips back to the barstool.

On the days when Stone had the afternoon shift, often at least one and sometimes even two or three girls would come in and ask if Charlie would be working that afternoon. When Stone said no they went away with an air of disappointment. Some were very good looking girls, some weren't. When Charlie came on for the evening shift and Stone told him about the girls being in to ask for him, Charlie would always say the same thing. "Christ," he would say and chuckle modestly.

He told Stone that after banging a girl he always had an uncontrollable desire to fall asleep, even if only briefly. Sometimes when Stone looked in on the taproom in late afternoon, he saw Charlie standing behind the bar, his head resting against the shelves, fast asleep standing up. It seemed safe to surmise that Charlie took more naps than anybody else at the whole resort.

Charlie had been an all-American lacrosse player in college but quit in his junior year, in late spring, just before final examinations, and had thereupon embarked upon a career of assorted jobs. "I hate to work," he told Stone, going on to say that he once had had a job as an Indian. Charlie smiled and shook his head. He was a used car salesman, he said, and the sales manager got the idea of having an advertising campaign to the effect that Big Chief Sam Rose was on the warpath against high prices, come see Big Chief Sam Rose and save plenty wampum. To make it all realistic, the manager wanted somebody to represent an Indian brave on the warpath against high prices and Charlie had to sit on top of a desk in the showroom with his legs crossed, wearing buckskin trousers, stripped to the waist and brandishing a tomahawk. "God-*dayum*," Charlie said reminiscently and then chuckled, noting that it hadn't turned out so bad because some of the women who saw him stripped to the waist called him up later in lieu of buying a car. Charlie clapped Stone hard on the shoulder and began laughing. "I tell you something, Jeff, I like to wore that old tommy-hawk of mine out."

For eating purposes the hotel help was divided into three categories which Stone, with bitter amusement, designated to himself as upstairs help—all white; downstairs white help; and colored help—all downstairs.

None of the help ate upstairs except Shirley and the other desk clerk, a girl named Joanie. They, both girls and both white, ate with Mr. Perry in the hotel dining room.

Stone's category was downstairs white help, which meant that he ate all his meals in the hotel basement, where they were cooked on an old stove with broken porcelain burner handles and eaten on a long wooden trestle-table of the sort that might be used by ranch hands.

Stone's eating campanions were Charlie and Joe and Mr. and Mrs. Gaston, all white. Joe was a lanky kid of about eighteen who set up umbrellas and beach chairs for the guests and who hated the food so much that he usually ate at the drug store. Mr. Gaston was the night clerk and Mrs. Gaston was his wife.

Both Gastons were getting on. Mr. Gaston looked about eighty and Mrs. Gaston about seventy. Mr. Gaston was a very meek, overly appreciative man with a very long face and a hooked nose and mild eyes. He looked like a hawk with thick white hair, but a very crestfallen hawk.

Mrs. Gaston's face was full of wrinkles and she wore rimless glasses with a sharp steel nose-piece that left a crease on the bridge of her nose. She was at the hotel only for the ride; that is, she was there with Mr. Gaston because he was night clerk and her board and room counted as part of his salary. She herself had no job, and Shirley told Stone that she sat

43

around all day in the lobby, listening intently to the conversations of the guests and sticking her nose into people's business, telling people she was from Dover, Delaware, which nobody seemed to find of much interest.

The Gastons were not happy with the eating arrangements, Mrs. Gaston in particular feeling they should have been permitted to eat upstairs in the hotel dining room. The arrangement downstairs was that the white help ate first, and then the colored help, at the same table, but only after the last of the downstairs white help had eaten and left, which they were supposed to do promptly. Mrs. Gaston sometimes deliberately took a long time to finish her coffee and generally dawdled. "Come along, Emma, time to finish up," Mr. Gaston would say gently. Mrs. Gaston would either ignore him or look resentfully at the black faces lined up behind the lattice that divided the dining space from the passageway. "I'm coming directly, Everett," she would reply with pique. "Give a person time to finish their coffee."

The downstairs dining room and kitchen were contained in the same large, airless, artificially lit room, and the entire operation was presided over, often tyrannically, by Lizzie, a colored woman of about sixty-five who was viewed by Mr. Perry as a relic of better times, perhaps old slave-times. Lizzie was a retired, or demoted, chambermaid who this summer had been assigned the job of downstairs cook, doubling as so-called bathhouse girl, because she was considered too old now to do chambermaid's work. Topheavy in appearance, dressed in drab colors, she went about in a sullen, pouting fury, most of which, Stone came to realize, was put on. When she became excited, which was often, she blinked her eyes rapidly and cocked her head, listening furiously to whatever was being said that excited her.

When there was something she didn't know or understand,

she became angry as a matter of course. "Who Hitler?" she once demanded of Stone, blinking and frowning.

Stone told her.

"He a white man?" she asked.

Stone said he was.

Still frowning, but less severely, she careened back to the stove.

Lizzie felt bad about not being a chambermaid any longer. When she wasn't cooking for the downstairs help, she sat on a bench outside the bathhouse and when the guests came down to the basement on their way out to the beach she would smile and laugh and simper and offer them a towel from the stack of clean towels she kept on the bench beside her. Then when they came in from the beach she would give them a cake of guest-size soap which she kept in a pasteboard box on the bench next to the towels.

She asked Stone if he would like a towel and Stone said no thanks, he wasn't going swimming just then. Lizzie touched her throat and said absently, "Gawd." Her eyes protruded and the eyelets of her heavy black shoes were mildewed. Anybody who slept in the basement was sure to have his personal belongings become mildewed. The shoes that Stone kept against the screen door to keep out the rats were badly mildewed, since he never wore them and they never saw the sun. Lizzie asked Stone why he never went swimming and he said he did occasionally. "Gawd," Lizzie said again and touched her throat, not listening.

When she was younger, Lizzie admitted to being the best chambermaid in the whole resort and possibly in the world. Shirley told Stone that Lizzie took particular pride in the speed with which she would clean a toilet. She called acid "assick" and Mr. Perry thought this was very funny. He told the guests and made the guests laugh. However, he was very fond of Lizzie, or said he was, pointing out that he had found a niche for her as downstairs cook doubling as bathhouse girl now that she was too old to be a chambermaid. He had assured her there would be a job for her so long as he had the hotel. Lizzie, however, seemed ashamed of herself for not being young enough to be a chambermaid any more. Sometimes Stone would see her looking morosely at the mildewed eyelets of her heavy black shoes.

Sometimes Stone found himself staring morosely at the ceiling of his dungeon room.

But he was not in his room nearly so often now. It had helped to come out and find as others before him had found, and as others after him would find, that it was all meaningless, all absurd.

* five

Shirley too he was determined to regard as unimportant, a person to whom he had no responsibility, a girl-clown who said funny things in a funny way, a sort of tomboy too tough ever to be hurt and so amusing that she was not to be taken seriously. Everything she said he tried steadfastly to view as funny. It entered his ear—and then before it reached his brain he converted it to his own purpose, telling himself that a funny person was beyond hurt.

"Hi, Stone, how's your place?" She was passing him in one of the underground passageways, headed for the stairway that led up to the lobby.

"What place?" he asked.

"The place where you got stuck by the bull." She grinned back at him over her shoulder and kept going.

Up early and determined to stay out of his dungeon, Stone went out and stood at the edge of the boardwalk. The beach was crowded with people lying in the sun, playing ball, flying kites, shrieking in the surf, all taking their pleasure without need to question its meaning. Stone sighed. He tucked his dark blue shirt into his white duck trousers and tightened his belt. From a steady diet of fried fish, sliced peaches and pink junket he had already lost weight.

"My God! Everywhere I go."

He turned. It was Shirley. He watched as she walked past to the mailbox, dropped in some letters and returned, smiling. "Hey, Stone, how do you like my new broomstick skirt?"

"Your what?"

Shirley pivoted and the skirt swirled. "See? You just wash it and then roll it up on a broomstick and it comes out all pleated, see?"

Stone nodded. "Great," he said. "As broomstick skirts go, it's a very nice broomstick skirt."

"Thanks." She turned and ran lightly up the front steps of the hotel.

Stone turned back to face the ocean. He tapped his stomach, feeling malnourished. He decided that he might like a milkshake but then, heading up the boardwalk toward the drug store, he wondered how he could be positive that he really wanted the milkshake. Seated at the soda fountain, he ordered one, spun a couple of times on the revolving seat, waited until the counter girl began to pour, and then watched intently as the foaming chocolate flowed smoothly from the aluminum shaker into the immaculate white paper cup.

For a few seconds he sat there, wondering whether, to him, there was any essential difference between drinking the milkshake and not drinking the milkshake. Then he drank it.

Stone was in the ladies room shaving when he heard the pad of bare feet along the passageway. "Hey!" Shirley had passed the open doorway but now turned back. "What in the hell are you doing in there, Stone?"

"Shaving," Stone said.

"Why in *there?*"

"Because it's where I always shave."

"Suppose somebody wants to come in?"

"Then I get out."

"Can I watch you shave?"

"I'm finished."

He slopped cold water on his face and came out, drying his neck with the sleeve of his shirt. Shirley had on a green gingham bathing suit. "Listen, Stone," she said, following him to his room, "why don't you come on out on the beach like a human being?"

"Is that what human beings do? Go out on beaches?"

"Oh, hell, Stone." Shirley sat on the edge of his cot and watched while he continued to dry his face, using now the pillow from his cot. "You act like you're a thousand years old. Why don't you ever come out on the beach?"

"I don't feel like it," he said.

"Why *don't* you feel like it? Getting stuck by a bull is no reason why you can't at least come out on the *beach.*" Shirley was now sprawled on his cot, her long tanned legs extended, one knee slightly bent. "Come on, Stone."

"No."

"Hey! I just realized something. You're not lying down. How come?"

"I never shave lying down."

"Okay, smart-ass. What I'm saying is that you don't lie down much any more. Why not?"

"I just don't, that's all."

"What do you think about when you're down here all by

yourself?"

"Nothing."

"Hah!" Shirley got up from the cot. "You're lying, Stone. Everybody has to be thinking about *something*. You can't *not*-think."

"So be it," Stone said. "Hey, let my damn pants alone."

Shirley was fishing around inside the orange crate, holding his spare pair of white ducks up by the belt loops. Carefully she folded them and put them back.

"I think a lot," she said. "I think about getting married to a really good guy this time and how he'll be just like a father to Laurie."

"That's nice," Stone said.

"You're not even listening. I'm leaving."

"Okay," Stone said.

"I'm not coming down to your lousy room any more. So you can forget it."

"Forget what?"

"It's all spoiled anyway."

"*What's* all spoiled anyway?"

"Go to hell, Stone," she said and left.

A couple of days later, Shirley got on Charlie's list, not on the barstool in the afternoon but in Shirley's bedroom late at night. Charlie told Stone about it the very next day. He said Shirley was okay, not-good-not-bad, except that she cried afterward and ran out of her own bedroom, leaving him there alone in her bed. Hardly knowing whether to fall asleep or not, Charlie took a very short nap and cleared out.

Shirley told Stone about it too. Even though she had vowed not to come down to his room any more she came down one night after supper and told him. Stone said he didn't want to hear about it.

"Why not?" Shirley demanded. "Why not, you bastard? Why not?"

"Because," Stone said. "Knowing about it is no different from *not* knowing about it."

"WHAT?"

Stone shrugged. "You heard me."

"Oh my God, no kidding," Shirley said. "You really are crazy, Stone, you really are."

She then told him how much she hated herself for going to bed with Charlie and Stone turned away, looking through the filthy screening that covered his window, seeing nothing.

"I *hate* Charlie," she said. "I *hate* that son of a bitch. Why did I do it?"

Staring through the screen, Stone shook his head. "Who knows?"

"A man can't have any idea," Shirley said.

"Any idea of what?"

"Any idea of what it's like to be married, and then suddenly *not* be married any more. It makes you horny, do you know what I mean, Stone? What in the hell are you looking at out there?"

"Nothing." Stone turned away from the window.

"I'll tell you something though," Shirley said. "Something you might just possibly like to hear. And that is that *you're much better than Charlie*. There wasn't even any comparison."

Stone felt something that he recognized as a warm glow of satisfaction. Sternly he nodded. "So be it," he said.

Next Shirley took to reading the Bible and came down to the taproom to announce it. "I've been doing a lot of reading myself lately," she said. "The Bible for instance."

She looked at him smugly, then told him that back in high school in Pennsylvania she had been elected Class Historian

50

of her graduating class, meaning, Stone supposed, that from this it naturally followed that some day she would begin studying the Bible.

He felt this was a clever observation but he passed up the opportunity to voice it because there was something about her that disturbed him. She wasn't being funny enough.

She was saying that her unfortunate surrender to Charlie might have been one of the best things that ever happened to her because it had made her see herself in all her enormity and now she could go on from there, which so far meant reading the Bible and thinking.

"That's nice," Stone said.

Now, she said, when she went out on the beach to get more suntan she at the same time had various *thoughts*. She would lie there on the blanket and think about her past life and she was beginning, she said, to think that maybe it was not entirely her ex-husband's fault, because what could you expect from a husband when the husband was only seventeen years old.

Even so, she went on, she still hated the little son of a bitch for hitting her, especially in the face where it showed. She also said that she had decided that if she were really pure in heart (as reading the Bible had inspired her to be) then she would stop calling her husband a son of a bitch, that this was one of the things she had figured out and what did Stone think.

Stone frowned. He found the way she was talking very strange, as if she were drunk but he knew she wasn't.

"You'd have to know the circumstances, I suppose," she said.

"I'd just as soon not know the circumstances," Stone said.

Shirley said that from now on she was going to ignore him when he made remarks like that because she knew he was crazy.

"You see, I was kind of wild in high school, even though I *was* elected Class Historian," she said, explaining that she was really elected Class Historian mainly because of the way she was built. "Does that surprise you?"

"Nothing surprises me," Stone said.

"Do *I* ever surprise you?"

Stone hesitated and then shook his head. "Nope."

Shirley was looking at him with sad eyes. "You know something, Stone? You know—"

And then she broke off because Charlie had come into the taproom even though he wasn't on duty.

Charlie had left his sunglasses on a shelf behind the bar. He wore only his swimming trunks, which were light blue and faded. Charlie had a lot of hair on his chest, which figured, and he was lean and lithe, which also figured, since he had been an all-American lacrosse player. Instead of going around behind the bar to get his sunglasses, he put his arm about Shirley's waist and said, "Hi there, sugar."

Stone saw Shirley stiffen. She sat there like a cake of ice in the shape of a girl, looking straight ahead, eyes smoky and blurred. Charlie put his hand under her chin and raised it; then, holding the point of her chin with one finger, he stood back and looked at her, grinning. Shirley just stared straight ahead, as if there weren't anybody holding up her chin with one finger at all. But there were puffs of pink beneath her eyes.

"Look at this, Stone," Charlie said. "What's the trouble, sugar?" Charlie removed his hand. "Cat got your tongue?" He started around behind the bar for his sunglasses, then asked Stone for them instead.

Stone passed the glasses to him across the bar, keeping his eyes on Shirley. Charlie put on his sunglasses. Jerking his head toward Shirley, he asked Stone, "What's wrong, she dead or something?"

Stone said nothing. Charlie left. Shirley came to life, just as if somebody had reached out and touched her with a wand. Except for the pink puffs beneath her eyes there was no sign that Charlie had even been there. She started talking about the Bible again, about the beatitudes, but then, right in the middle of a beatitude, she broke off, let go with a stream of obscenity, and told Stone he was as big a bastard as Charlie. Then she left.

That evening after eating his supper in the downstairs help's dining room, Stone went in and lay on his cot for a while, thinking.

Then he went into the taproom and when there was a lull in business he asked Charlie to step back into the storeroom.

"What's up?" Charlie asked, looking beleaguered.

Stone shrugged. "Hell," he said. "Nothing. What I'm going to ask you doesn't even make any sense, as far as that's concerned. But—don't take Shirley out and lay her any more, okay?"

Charlie was aggrieved. "Why? You layin' her, Stone? Hell, man, she don't mean a thing to me. Course I won't lay her any more if you say so. Shake?"

Charlie gave Stone his boyish grin, bringing out the cleft in his chin and the dimples in his cheeks. He was holding out his hand.

Stone shook it. "Hell," he said, "it doesn't make any difference to me one way or the other, so far as that goes."

"What doesn't? Charlie asked.

"Whether you lay her or don't lay her."

Charlie looked puzzled. "What the hell—you just said—"

"So you might as well not lay her," Stone said.

"Good deal," Charlie said, giving Stone a friendly clap on the shoulder. "Buddies?"

Stone nodded.

✳ six

Stone wished that Shirley hadn't felt so humiliated about going to bed with Charlie. If she had been cool and sophisticated about it he would have felt better.

After bolting from the taproom in the midst of the beatitudes, she didn't show up for a couple of days, and Stone had the feeling that she was avoiding him, which of course was just as well.

On the third day he had the afternoon shift. Business in the taproom was slack and the afternoon dragged. For a while he amused himself by wadding the bar rag into a ball and throwing it into the air and catching it. Every now and then he found himself looking expectantly at the slitted windows, and he realized that what he expected to see was a glimpse of Shirley's legs as she passed the window on her way to the outside stairs that led down to the taproom.

When she came down it was after five o'clock. He was back in the storeroom and didn't know she was there until she called to him. She was sitting on a barstool, dressed for evening in something he had never seen before, a white dress with a floppy collar that gave the impression of a middy-blouse. For some reason it made her look about fourteen instead of twenty-one.

He was very relieved to find that she had gotten over feeling sad and angry about Charlie. She was blithe and flippant, talking half-seriously of her bouts with the Bible and even relating the scriptures to Charlie.

"Do you think Charlie will get his just deserts?" she asked,

54

Stone smiled. "What would they be exactly?"

"Don't you think something is liable to happen to him?"

"I guess so," Stone said. "Exhaustion maybe."

He found that something about her was getting to him tonight, perhaps the little-girl sailor dress, perhaps the extreme fragility of her wrists as they lay helpless on the bar. He decided that he had better muster up his reserve of indifference.

"Would you consider Charlie poor in spirit?" she asked.

Stone shrugged. He said he didn't know what poor in spirit meant, looking all the while at her wrists, wondering what there was about them, or about him.

"Well, would you consider him meek?"

Stone deliberated. "I'm not sure."

"Are you *serious?*" She shook her head. "He's about as far from being *meek* as anybody I ever knew. *You're* sort of meek, Jeff."

"Thanks," Stone said. He looked into her eyes. She looked back at him, blinking, and he had a strong impression of bravado, although he wasn't sure.

"My Uncle Jack was a very meek man," she said. "You should have known my Uncle Jack, Jeff. He didn't hit my Aunt Esther once, the whole time they were married, at least not in the face, I know that for a fact."

Stone turned away and picked up a glass to polish. "That's nice," he said.

"You'd have liked him."

She went on to say that her Uncle Jack wasn't content to work in the mines like the others but went off to live in Philadelphia and wore suits.

Stone chuckled. "That's nice," he said.

"Is that your idea of something funny?"

"*You're* my idea of something funny," he said.

"Well good for me. I'm funny."

Shirley slid from the barstool. "You know something, Jeff? You're kind of funny yourself. Did you ever think of that?"

She walked over to the juke box and abruptly, although she had played no record, she began a series of frenzied jitterbug steps in her bare feet, reminding him of some photographs Life Magazine had run of the Savoy Ballroom in Harlem.

Panting, she returned to the bar. "How did you like *that*, Stone?"

"That was very good, Shirley. I like your dress."

"Do you? Well good for me. You think I'm funny and you like my dress. Tell me something, Stone. Did your father ever hit *your* mother?"

Stone was aware that his lower teeth had come up hard against his upper teeth. For an instant he was looking at his mother's face, seeing the pale freckles beneath her eyes. "Not that I know of," he said.

"Not once? *Never?*"

Stone said not that he knew of. He then opened himself a bottle of beer, something he did only rarely, taking a quarter from his pocket and ringing up the quarter on the cash register.

"You know . . ." Shirley said. "Some of the miners' wives *like* getting hit. They get a sexual thrill out of it. But I never could."

Stone drank his beer, looking again at the frailty of her wrists and then away.

Shirley was playing with her cigarette lighter, staring off into space, as if deep in thought, and then looked quickly about the taproom to make sure they were still alone. "Remember the night we went up the beach, Jeff . . ."

"Yes," Stone said uncomfortably.

"Remember *afterward* . . . and I was looking around for my pants . . . because I was getting chilly?"

"Yes," Stone said. "What about it?"

"And you had kept them in your pocket—you'd kept them in your pocket for me?"

Stone nodded. "What about it?"

"Nothing. I just thought it was nice. It sort of reminded me of my Uncle Jack. It was sort of, you know . . . sort of considerate."

"You mean that's what your Uncle Jack would have done?"

"I don't know. I'm just saying. In a certain way you remind me of my Uncle Jack. That's all." Shirley sighed and lit and re-lit her cigarette lighter. "That was a beautiful, night, Stone. Really."

Stone said nothing.

"Really," Shirley said again. For a while longer she played with her cigarette lighter, then snapped it shut. "My—"

Stone waited. "Your what?"

"My Uncle Jack was my favorite uncle," she said, and there were tears in her eyes. She looked up at him, blinking rapidly.

"For God's sake, Shirley . . ."

She shook her head. "I don't give a damn about you, Stone, because you're a stupid dumb bastard."

"I probably am," he said.

"I know you'd never marry anybody dumb like I am," she said, "but boy, what a wife I'd be to you, Stone. I'd really *fight* for you. I'd *kill* anybody who tried to hurt you."

"My God. Shirley! I can't marry you. I can't marry *anybody*. I'm about to go into the damned army. Besides, I'm a wreck, I'm all bitched up, I really am."

Shirley nodded, looking sadly down at the bar, sadly at her cigarette lighter. "I know," she said. "You've been gored. So you'd like to have this sad, wistful relationship.

"So what's wrong with that?"

"What's wrong with *anything?*" she said. "What's wrong with me leaving Laurie all summer? What's wrong with me screwing Charlie when I love *you?*"

"Are you worried about her?"

"Of *course* I'm worried about her. God knows what's going on back there. By now my father may have started hitting *her* in the face, that bastard. Every night when I go to sleep I think about it and I almost go crazy. If he does I'll kill him."

"Your father?"

"Yes. My father. The bastard, I'll kill him—listen, if you come near me with that stinking thing again, Stone, so help me I'm going to wrap it around your neck."

Stone had grabbed up his bar rag and was swabbing aimlessly. He threw it on the floor. "I'm sorry." He took a deep breath. "Listen, Shirley, I've got to be honest. I can be your friend. I can be a damned good friend but that's all I can be. And it doesn't mean I don't find you attractive. What else can I say?"

"Nothing." Shirley was smiling down at the bar again. "Nothing, Jeff. That's all you can say."

"God!" Stone said. "Sometimes I get the impression that you came down here just to get a husband. That your mother's taking care of Laurie for the summer just so you'll be free to look."

Shirley laughed. "That's brilliant of you, Stone."

"No, I mean no kidding. That you're determined to get *some* kind of husband by the end of the summer regardless."

"That's close," she said.

"Are you serious?"

"Yes, I'm serious. What do you want me to do—be coy?"

"Even if you don't love him?"

"Oh, God, Stone, you're so stupid for your age, you really are. I need somebody, don't you understand? Otherwise I go back home and spend the rest of my life being a bag girl in the

A & P, with a three-year-old daughter to take care of."

"But why does it have to be right now? This summer?"

"Because this is the last summer I'll ever have. I can't let my mother take care of Laurie again, even if she would."

"Why not?"

Shirley's eyes blazed. "Because I *love* her, you damned fool. And I don't like to be away from her. I *miss* her."

"Whew!" Stone let out his breath and began to do a few clog steps behind the bar.

"What in the hell are you *doing?*"

"Nothing," Stone said. "You mean when the summer ends you're going to have a husband? *Some* husband?"

"Maybe." Shirley smiled sadly. "Maybe not. It would be silly to say for certain that I was."

"Well, don't you see how lousy it would be of me to mess around with you and monopolize your time?"

She nodded.

"Hell," Stone said, "maybe I can help you . . . find one."

"That would be very nice of you, Stone. Very very—"

She looked up at him, blinking rapidly, and then lowered her face to the bar. Stone touched the top of her head. "Oh, God, Shirley . . ." He patted her hair. "There's nothing to *cry* about."

Her chin was resting in a puddle of foam from the beer he had opened. Raising her chin with one hand, he wiped up the puddle. Then, with his finger and thumb, he encircled her wrist, raising it and kissing it.

She blinked at him. "Who's crying, you bastard?" She wiped her eyes with her knuckles and then in her bare feet padded from the room.

When Charlie came on to relieve him, Stone went to his room and lay on his cot, looking up at the ceiling where he had punched the holes with his fist on the night of his incredible sunburn. Finally he got up and went in for supper but he was very late. The downstairs colored help were all seated at the table. There was space for him, so he sat dazedly next to William but then almost immediately he felt knuckles against the side of his head and Lizzie was listing heavily above him, head cocked, batting her eyes furiously. "Get up from there, boy. Get *up* from there. Mr. Perry see you there he'll kill you and me both." She kept jabbing him on the arm, shoving him ahead of her out into the passageway while the older ones let out whoops of laughter and the younger ones barely chuckled. Out in the passageway, Lizzie said, "You come back in a half hour, Jeff, I'll fix you something nice." She patted his shoulder and careened back to her post.

Stone returned to his room and lay on his cot. He tried to whistle Lester Young's saxophone chorus from *Honeysuckle Rose*, which he knew note for note, but now, in the darkness, it came out all thin and flat and lousy.

So he stopped whistling and just lay there in the dark.

∗ seven

Stone's father called to say he would be in the area on a business trip toward the end of the week and naturally would stop by to say hello and maybe have a dip in the ocean. He asked Stone how things were going and Stone said things were going okay. His father said the Russians were putting up quite a fight so far and Stone agreed that they were. His father said, "Okay, then," and Stone said, "Okay, fine."

When Stone was very young, five or six, he had been sent to visit his paternal grandparents and he had slept in a small room, alone. In the middle of the night, when the house was quiet and dark, he awoke from a bad dream. He had dreamed that his father was dead. Stricken with grief and fear, he turned on the light, seeing his father's picture, with its sensual mouth and the stiff collar and the necktie with its huge knot. Later, when he knew about Scott Fitzgerald, he would think that one reminded him of the other. But then, at the age of five or six, he had looked at his father's picture, remembering the nightmare, and thought, with tears in his eyes, what a fine man, some day that fine man will die. Thinking about it later, he realized he had been quite young to have thought such a thing but he knew for a fact that he had been no more than six. He had thought it and whispered it and then, choked with grief, sobbed aloud, "What a fine man, some day that fine man will die."

Stone was sprawled on his cot after lunch when his father came in and grasped his hand very hard. As they shook hands, Stone looked his father in the eye, seeing there a mixture of affection and wariness, then Stone looked down at the dirty base of the large white pillar.

His father changed into his swimming trunks, spreading his clothes out neatly on Stone's cot, and they went out to the beach. As his father jumped from the boardwalk down to the sand, Stone saw him glance northward as if he were trying to see a long distance. His father then looked down at the sand, circling a few steps, looking for the place where he thought he might best sit. Stone circled as his father circled, feeling the barrier between them.

Finally they were seated and his father tried to pierce the barrier with an old and trusted barrier-piercer, noting in a

61

hearty voice that Joe DiMaggio's consecutive game hitting streak was still in progress, while Ted Williams, for his part, might very likely finish the season batting over .400 if he kept hitting the way he was hitting. His father asked Stone which he considered the better hitter and Stone said he wasn't sure, Williams probably, if it was just batting average his father was talking about. His father said he was inclined to agree.

A few hundred feet offshore, flying low, a small biplane towed a red streamered sign reading, "Movie Tonite, Rebecca."

Stone's father sat with his arms outthrust behind him, fingers curled in the sand. He was looking off to sea, following the flight of the plane with pleasure and even excitement. Stone was taller than his father and slimmer and of course much tanner. His father tanned poorly. If he stayed in the sun for more than a couple of hours his skin became the shade of pink junket. Now his body was white and there was a modest role of fat resting on the waistband of his bright blue swimming trunks. From knee to ankle his legs were not so hairy as Stone remembered them. His legs were rather slim for his weight, the legs of a sprinter. His shoulders were very broad, covered by a mass of freckles which over the years had joined to form a solid yoke. People said his father was handsome and Stone supposed he was. His hair was still thick, just beginning to grey at the temples, for his father was still quite young, twenty-one years older than Stone, which made him now forty-three and this, as fathers of grown sons went, was quite young. In his eyes, as he continued to follow the flight of the plane, there was a look of boyish eagerness, and Stone realized that he could not say it was a new look, not something he could blame on Ellen, for his father had had the same boyish look ever since he could remember. But when his eyes left the plane and turned again to Stone there was, again, a wary glint, as if his father were determined that his eagerness was not going to be spoiled by the melancholy of a stern son.

His father said that since he was still hot and grimy from the automobile ride down he thought he would take a dip and cool off. Stone watched as his father trotted toward the surf on his sprinters' legs and then picked up speed, running through the shallow water and launching his chunky body in a flat dive, bursting through the green wall of a wave, emerging in the calm water beyond, shaking his head and fingering his eyes. He began to swim with slow, powerful strokes. Stone picked up a handful of sand and let it sift slowly between his fingers. He realized it gave him pleasure that his father swam well.

His father stayed in the water only a few minutes. When he came out he wiped the water from his eyes, dried his hands, and lit a cigarette. "Boy!" he said. "That was a real work-out!"

Sitting on a towel, he said that he had run across a magazine article entitled, "Off to the Service in the Right Frame of Mind." He said he thought Stone would find the article quite interesting, that it had struck a responsive chord when he himself read it, since in World War I he had spent almost a year in the navy, sleeping the entire while in a hammock.

Stone asked what frame of mind the article was recommending, and his father said it urged draftees not to get themselves all churned up. Stone nodded and then asked what the article suggested as an alternative to getting all churned up. His father said Stone could read it for himself, that he still had it somewhere around the office and would mail it when he got back to the city.

Stone noticed how indiscriminate his father's conversation was. He seemed willing and ready to talk about anything at all, and the less relevant the topic the more at ease he seemed. Stone listened in silence, and he wondered if perhaps he was deliberately, from sheer disappointment and anger, letting his father ramble from topic to topic, waiting for his father to say something he could adjudge stupid.

His father was speaking of the junior life-saving courses his brothers were now taking at the public pool. Stone was looking toward the water's edge, watching a child dig in the wet sand, but he was thinking of the track shoes and basketball his father had bought him, as well as the shoulder pads, in the heart of the depression when there was no money for shoulder pads; and thinking of the feeling of closeness engendered when, in his early teens, several years in a row, he and his father had worked together in the weeks before Christmas on a new electric train layout, once painting an old bedspread green and stuffing it with newspapers to simulate a mountain and tunnel. He thought of all the hours and hours his father had spent working on it and of the eager enthusiasm his father had had for the mountain and tunnel.

Now his father was talking of the infrequency of thunderstorms that summer. Watching the kid digging in the sand, Stone listened to what his father was saying and felt his face twist with disbelief and disgust.

His father turned his head to look in the direction of a huge clock that adorned the facade of one of the nearby hotels. "Usually," he said, "even in a hot spell, you can count on a few thunderstorms to bring a little relief."

Stone nodded. Clutching a handful of sand tight, he said, "I've been thinking a lot about you and mother." It surprised him to realize how choked up he felt even to say that much.

His father glanced at him warily and then looked to the north. "I hate for you to worry about that sort of thing, Jeff," he said. "What I want you to do, what your mother and I *both* want you to do, is just enjoy your summer down here—where it's cool."

Stone let the sand sift slowly over his knee. "I have to

worry about it," he said. His voice broke, and he picked up more sand. "I have no choice. It's very important to me."

He hoped his father would hear and recognize the change in his voice, the call for truce, the call for closeness, the invitation to reason; that his father would hear the note of pleading so that he would not have to plead with words, for he knew he could no more plead with words than he could tell his father about finding the note in the pocket of his bathrobe. "I've been thinking about the economics of it," Stone said.

"Economics?" His father seemed to brighten. "Yes, well I guess it's natural that you might. But what do economics have to do with it?"

To his amazement, Stone realized that even now his father could take time out to feel pleasure and pride in remembering that economics had been his major, for it reminded him that he had put a son through college.

"I've been sort of analyzing it," Stone said, looking at the sand. "In terms of economics. Because I think it's true that economics underlie much of human behavior. I mean, you and mother got married when you were both very young. You were only twenty and she was only nineteen . . ."

Stone found it painful to get the words out. He kept fearing that any minute his voice would break. "And then," he said, "you had kids so early, so that right off the bat you were sort of chained to a job, only twenty-six or twenty-seven, with a wife and three kids to support. And you did a . . ." Stone closed his eyes, fighting for control of his voice, hoping it would not break. ". . . darn good job of it."

His father was looking out over the ocean. His eyes were clouded. "I've never minded working hard for you boys," he said softly.

"How about for Mother?"

"Not for your mother either," his father said.

Stone nodded, feeling relief and pleasure, because he had not expected to hear his father say, "Not for your mother either."

"I think maybe I've had just about enough sun," his father said. "Aren't you going in for a dip?"

"I don't think so," Stone said, "I—" He paused, trying to find the words in the popsicle wrapper that he had dug from the sand and now held between his fingers. "The first ten years of your marriage were the 'twenties, and second ten more or less covered the 'thirties with the depression and everything. I mean, it's only been in the last couple of years or so, since the recession ended, that you've felt what it was like to have any extra money."

"That's true, that part of it," his father said. "But I just don't see—"

"What I'm trying to say," Stone went on, "is that now that you do have some money you feel sort of like you want to sort of—*burst forth.*" He had raised his eyes to his father's and raised his voice, so that the last two words themselves had burst forth. He looked down again at the sand. "I mean, it's only natural—economically. Anybody would."

He looked up at his father, appealing with his eyes, but his father was not looking at him. He was getting up and brushing the sand from his trunks. "Jeff," he said. "I just don't want you to worry about such things. Whatever problems your mother and I have, we'll work them out between ourselves, and there's one thing you can be darn sure of, and that is that what I feel for you boys will never ever change. Not one bit."

His father was still brushing the sand from his trunks and then from his shins and ankles. "I appreciate your concern. I appreciate your caring, Jeff."

His father straightened. Grabbing the hem of his trunks, he twisted but no water dripped. They were about dry. "I think if I stay out there in the sun much longer though I'll live to regret it. So I think I should go in and have a shower. It's almost four-thirty. Is there a shower I can use below-decks somewhere?"

Stone was staring out over the ocean. He didn't answer.

His father walked off a few steps. Again he wrung the hem of his trunks, and returned. "Jeff . . . is there a shower in the hotel I could use?"

Stone nodded. He said there was and that he would show him the way.

"Is there always this good a breeze?" his father asked.

Stone said there was, normally.

"Well . . ." His father gave him what Stone later would regard as a shrewd look. Then he said in an offhand way that there was someone he would like Stone to meet, a Mrs. Hopper, who was staying at one of the hotels at the north end of the beach.

He said he felt sure Stone would like her, adding that he felt obliged to say hello to her because she was the wife of one of his very best customers.

He suggested that Stone might want to fix himself up a bit.

✳ eight

With his white ducks and dark blue sports shirt, Stone wore a seersucker jacket and in late afternoon they strode north-ward along the boardwalk.

Stone's father's face was aglow from his time in the sun.

His hair was parted crisply. Instead of the clothes he had spread out on Stone's cot, he wore a white linen suit with floppy pants which he had taken from the car.

Mrs. Hopper, his father said, was staying at The Galleon, one of the hotels at the wealthy end of the beach. It looked Spanish, with dark yellow stucco and a lot of arches.

As they entered the lobby, Mrs. Hopper came forward to meet them. Mrs. Hopper had eyes of green glass, rimmed in black. Her dark hair was parted in the middle and she looked not unlike Dolores del Rio, except for a snub nose.

Eyes shining, she held out her hand to his father. "Hi," his father said. "It's nice to see you. I'd like you to meet my son. Jeff, this is Mrs. Hopper."

"How do you *do*, Jeff . . . ?" She seemed to draw back as if better to appraise him, and the effect was of admiration.

On the patio in front of her hotel they sat at a round table. Stone's back was to the ocean. He sat facing the hotel, looking into its dining room through the broad arches. The dining room was open to the air and to long diagonal slants of sunlight from the west. Small birds hopped along the paths of light, in search of crumbs.

Mrs. Hopper was looking into Stone's eyes. "Jeffrey," she said intensely, "it's so nice to *meet* you." Her voice was shrill. It did not go with her face. "I've heard so much about you from your father . . ." She laughed. Her laugh was horrible. But she was stacked, and she had very good legs, so deeply tanned that her shinbones gleamed.

Nodding at what she was saying, Stone tried to relax, telling himself that he could not be at all certain that Mrs. Hopper was necessarily *Ellen* Hopper.

Stone heard the drone of the plane and they all turned, watching the small biplane that was still tugging the streamered sign advertising the movie. Mrs. Hopper asked Stone if he had seen *Rebecca* and he said no, he hadn't. Mrs. Hopper said she had seen it three times, once about a year ago when it first came out and twice since, having always been fond of Laurence Olivier. Stone's father said he seldom went to the movies because he was too busy. From a waitress he ordered Scotch for himself and cokes for Mrs. Hopper and Stone.

Then, turning to Mrs. Hopper, his father said, "Have you been down here long . . . Ellen?"

Stone watched the birds hopping along the path of sunlight. He felt his face grow hot and wondered if they were noticing how hot his face was.

The word, the name, hung in the air.

Stone reminded himself that hearing the word was no different from not hearing the word, and then he was telling himself not to be a damned fool because there had never been any doubt about it, and then thinking that since Ellen existed she might as well be this woman as some other woman.

He sat rigidly, watching the birds.

"Yes," Mrs. Hopper was saying. "I've been here almost two weeks, and I'll be here until the end of August."

"Well then you might as well say you're spending the whole summer . . ." His father said this and then laughed far too heartily for the merit of his own observation.

Mrs. Hopper was nervous and so was his father. They both talked steadily and Mrs. Hopper nodded with great animation even though what his father said wasn't anything to be animated about.

Stone listened, feeling now much older than his father. He wondered why she had come down to the beach, why she had picked *this* beach, yet he knew that if she was going to spend time at the beach then this would be the beach she would pick, since it was the only ocean resort within 400 miles.

He knew now why his father had kept looking northward. And he knew that on the day he had taken his long walk, his father was the man he had seen ducking behind the umbrella.

69

Stone sat there feeling paralyzed, sat stiffly in his seersucker jacket, feeling as if two huge and powerful hands were pressed tight to his head, holding it prisoner, forcing him to remain motionless and silent, forcing him to watch the birds that searched for crumbs.

"Has there been a good crowd down at your hotel this summer, Jeffrey?" Mrs. Hopper asked.

Stone said the crowd had seemed pretty good to him. He cleared his throat and sipped his coke.

Mrs. Hopper, he thought, and his mouth moved. It was a perfect name for a mistress. Frozen, he sat trying to think of more appropriate first names than Ellen. Mary Ann Hopper, he thought. *Hurry* Ann Hopper.

He knew that he was presenting a poor appearance, awkward, catatonic, but he didn't care and would have been unable to do anything about it even if he had cared. He sat looking into the recesses of the dining room as if the dining room were of enormous interest, raising his eyes briefly now and then to Ellen Hopper's face and then looking down at her glittering shinbones and several times at the jagged thrust of her breasts against the green linen sleeveless dress. He had been asked a question.

"Yes." He cleared his throat and said again, this time in a ringing voice, "Yes. I have all my mornings off, so I can get out on the beach quite a bit. No, I haven't left since I got here. I don't have a car."

"There's not much point in having one," his father said. "I guess you read what Mr. Ickes had to say . . . about jackrabbit starts. Anybody caught revving up his motor and squealing his tires and so forth is going to get fined for wasting gasoline."

Mrs. Hopper was looking shrewdly at Stone, who could tell from the corner of his eye that this was what she was doing.

Now she was talking about sombeody who had given her-self and her husband some gasoline rationing stamps. "Yes," she said to his father. "Gave them to he and I together."

Staring at the birds, Stone felt his lip raise with contempt. Stupid bitch, he thought with satisfaction. She doesn't even know grammar.

And God, what a laugh she had, he thought, as her shrill, raucous laugh rang out at something unfunny his father had said. How stupid he had been a few minutes earlier to think, it may as well be this woman as some other woman.

The wind had died, which it often did toward evening, and his father commented upon it because his father had become fond of commenting upon the wind. His father's face was still glowing. It looked carefully brushed to bring up the circulation. Spotted here and there in the glow of his sunburn were faint red and blue flecks in his cheeks and nose. With his white linen suit he wore a blue shirt and a red-and-blue striped tie. There were rose and blue edges to the clouds that drifted out over the ocean. There was rosy expectation in his father's eyes. Mrs. Hopper looked closely at Stone but when he looked back at her she looked away, asking him how he liked his bartending job. She said she would drop in for a coke some time, having always her entire life hated beer.

His father said he had never much cared for beer either, preferring Scotch. Mrs. Hopper said her own preference was bourbon. Stone, looking at his watch, said it was time for him to get back.

His father told Stone to show Mrs. Hopper his watch, which his father and mother had given him for graduation. "That was his graduation present," his father said. Mrs. Hopper said it was a beautiful watch. Holding Stone's hand, she looked into his eyes. Stone dropped his hand and then his eyes to his lap.

Mrs. Hopper asked if they wouldn't like to have supper

right there at her hotel, since they were both already there anyway, and Stone said he didn't have time, that all he had time for was a very quick supper, which he got as part of his salary and hence might as well eat.

His father said he'd stay on and finish his drink and that he had to leave for the city soon but that in any event he would drop by the taproom and say goodbye before he left.

Stone walked back down the boardwalk, eyes straight ahead, feeling numb.

Well, whaddya think? he asked of Christ. *It's a tough go,* Christ replied.

It was after nine o'clock when his father came down to the taproom and took a seat on a barstool, still resplendent in his still crisp linen siut. He said it was time for him to get on back to the city, back home. In his eyes the look of wariness was more pronounced, as if he were ready to flinch if need be.

"Any message you'd like me to give your mother?" he asked.

Stone looked at him briefly and then turned away, feeling contempt. He opened two bottles of beer and served two customers, took their money and rang it up on the cash register, wiped the counter vigorously with the bar cloth. "Not that I can think of," he said.

"Well . . . I'll be getting along then," his father said, going on to say that it had been good to see him and that he had enjoyed their talk and the swim and appreciated the use of the shower and that Mrs. Hopper had thought he was very nice.

Stone nodded. He gave his father a shrewd look and then, in an offhand way, asked how old Mrs. Hopper was.

"She's about thirty-seven I'd say," his father said. "Why?" He seemed pleased that Stone had asked.

"No reason," Stone said. "I just wondered."

Coming out from behind the bar, he followed his father to the doorway that led up one flight of steps to the side street. "I just wanted to say one more thing," he said.

"What about?" His father turned, on guard.

"About the stuff we were talking about on the beach," Stone said. "This is what I've been thinking. About the gravy boat. Let's say she *did* ignore your wishes. Let's even say she did it deliberately, which I very much doubt."

His father frowned. He looked uncomfortable. His pants seemed baggier. He looked quickly at Stone and then over his shoulder at the four customers lined up at the bar, and at the scattering of those at the tables.

"It was up to *you* to make her *not* ignore your wishes," Stone said, choking up.

His father shook his head. "I don't want to talk about it here, Jeff. We'll talk about it some other time. I don't agree with you but I'm willing to talk about it—some other time."

"If you wanted to preserve the marriage and the family," Stone said, lowering his voice, "then it was up to you to prevent anything that *threatened* the marriage and the family. With the force of your will. Because you're the *head* of the family."

His father's face had grown hard. He shook his head. "I just don't see it that way," he said. "But this is certainly not the time and place—"

"If Mother didn't buy a new gravy boat, then you should have *made* her buy a new gravy boat, damn it," Stone said savagely. "Besides, you know damn well it *wasn't* the gravy boat anyway." Then he said no more because his voice had broken and he could not trust it.

"Son . . ."

Stone turned away, not wanting his father to see his eyes. His father touched him briefly on the shoulder, then grabbed a handful of shoulder and squeezed.

Then his father was gone.

When Stone went back to his post behind the bar he felt uncoordinated. As he uncapped a bottle of beer, his hand shook.

When Mr. Perry came down at midnight and found the beer was eleven bottles short, Stone nodded numbly. "It's gotta stop," Mr. Perry said and stomped out.

Stone closed the taproom and went in and lay on his cot in his white ducks and blue shirt. Over the orange crate hung his seersucker jacket.

Presently he heard William come in next door. "Hey, man," William called softly.

Stone didn't answer. He turned over and lay face down.

✳ nine

On July 10, 1941, there was a lull all along the German-Russian front, and the Red Army appeared to have fought the Germans to a standstill.

On the same day, Charlie broached the idea of holding a taproom beauty contest. He asked Stone what he thought.

Stone was working the afternoon shift. He looked up from a newspaper which he had spread on top of the bar. Charlie had just come in from the beach, wearing only his faded blue swim trunks, dripping water on the floor.

"Why?" Stone asked.

Charlie said it would give the taproom publicity, which would be good for business.

Stone, glancing down at his newspaper, said he felt that Charlie was already giving the taproom a lot of publicity, singlehanded.

Charlie explained that he meant *public* publicity.

He said that if it worked out they could have a taproom beauty contest every week, with the top of the bar as runway. He asked Stone what he thought.

Stone looked up at the ceiling, measuring the distance with his eyes. He said the ceiling was too low and that if the girls stood on the bar they would bump their heads.

Charlie was forced to admit that this was true. "Maybe they could bend over a little," he said.

"Ummm," Stone said doubtfully.

Charlie asked Stone to suggest the beauty contest idea to Mr. Perry but Stone said that since it was his idea he should be the one to suggest it to Mr. Perry. Charlie said he would see what he could work out.

One of Charlie's many friends was a man named Les, who was editor of *The Resorter*, a newspaper of sorts which came out twice weekly, printing mostly names. Starting with the left hand column on the front page, it would say: "Staying at the Atlantis Hotel this week were:"—and then would list the name and home town of every person registered that week at the Atlantis Hotel. It would then do the same, in alphabetical order, for all the other hotels, until there were no more names to print, or no more space in which to print them. Usually the front page featured a photograph of some guy posing next to a marlin he had caught while deep-sea fishing. The caption was always the same—"Catches Marlin."

Charlie got Les to promise to help out with the publicity for the beauty contest and only then did he approach Mr. Perry, telling him it would be very good for business and convincing him in short order.

The beauty contest was held on a Sunday afternoon.

Charlie had rounded up about ten girls, each of whom would be required to display some special talent to go along with her beauty.

There was a fair crowd on hand, including Mr. Perry and Shirley and Lizzie, as well as Stone, who stood behind the bar.

Lizzie hung back just inside the storeroom, looking out and batting her eyes with excitement.

In the talent part of the contest, several of the girls did the Suzy-Q, two turned cartwheels and another whistled *Indian Love Call.*

The judges were Charlie, Les, and the Captain of the Life Guards. Mr. Perry was an Honorary Judge.

Charlie explained that there would be The Winner, who woud be crowned Miss Utopia; and then a First Runnerup and a Second Runnerup.

The winner was supposed to have her picture on the front page of the newspaper, in the space where the marlin usually appeared.

Each of the judges voted for a different winner, whereupon Les and the Captain of the Life Guards started a bitter argument. The Captain of the Life Guards told Les he ran a lousy newspaper and threatened to punch him in the nose. The Captain of the Life Guards was a mass of heavily tanned brawn and Les was about five feet eight. Mr. Perry exclaimed, "Here! We can't have this kind of thing going on, I happen to own this place lock-stock-and-barrel."

Mr. Perry, as Honorary Judge, then cast the tie-breaking vote, and the winner turned out to be an eighteen-year-old girl from Smyrna, Delaware, named Mary Crankshaw who, upon being interviewed by Les, divulged that she loved the Suzy-Q, the Big Apple and had a twelve-year-old brother.

She and her Court of Honor stood on the bar slightly hunched and had their pictures taken. Charlie then lingeringly lifted each in turn to the floor, taking a good long time about it, and they lined up in front of the bar and had some more pictures taken, trucking.

Lizzie had come out of the taproom and was standing next to Stone. Without realizing what he was doing, Stone began patting Lizzie's shoulder, whereupon Lizzie batted her eyes, scowled, and retreated into the storeroom again.

All agreed that the contest had been by and large a success, and all the spectators were then invited by Mr. Perry to step up to the bar and refresh themselves at their own expense.

On Tuesday, *The Resorter* came out with a picture of the girl who won the beauty contest. Under the picture, it said, "Mary Crankshaw Lissome, Smyrna, Del., girl who won beauty contest on Sunday at the Utopia Bar and Grill."

The caption above the picture said, "Catches Marlin."

✳ ten

Stone by now had returned to the dark comfort of his room, and once more the real things of the world were the huge white pillar, the orange crate, the dull orange light and the black window with its view of nothing.

The unreal things included his father.

Dear Dad, he would write. *I realize . . .*

Dear Dad, Even though you say . . .

Dear Dad, I'm writing this with the hope . . .

Stone frowned. "What?" he asked.

"I said I'm willing to be your friend, Jeff, if that's the way you want it."

Shirley was sitting on the floor next to his cot, her right arm resting on the edge of the mattress, her cheek pressed to her arm, the orange light falling on her hair. He touched her hair with his palm, pressing down a little, and then took his hand away. He realized that he no longer wished she had kept her waitress job at the south end of the boardwalk.

"Okay," he said.

"It makes me feel good to be with you," she said.

"Okay. I'm glad it does."

"Do you like it when I'm with you, Jeff?"

"Yes," he said. "I like it when you're with me."

"So long as I'm not hustling you . . ."

"Yes."

"And you are my friend?"

"Yes. I'll be your friend until you find a husband." Smiling, he patted her head. "Maybe I *can* help you find a husband, if that's what you want . . . I mean, if you'd rather have a husband than work in the A & P."

"You've already helped me, Jeff. I feel better. I like myself better than I used to."

"That's good, Shirley."

"You know what you are, Jeff? You're idealistic. That's what I've decided."

He laughed. "Is that what you've decided?"

"Yep." Getting to her feet, she leaned over the cot and kissed his forehead. "Okay, if I'm going to be your friend there's something I should tell you. Except you won't like it."

"What is it?"

Shirley backed against the pillar and looked down at him somberly. "Mr. Perry is suspicious of you."

"*What?*"

"He thinks you're the one responsible for the shortages in the taproom."

"My God! How about *Charlie?*"

She said that Mr. Perry looked upon Charlie with new respect since the beauty contest, that he considered Charlie imaginative and forward-looking.

"And do you know something else?" Shirley asked.

"What?"

"Mr. Perry is crazy."

Stone nodded. "Yeah. I already knew that."

"But I mean *really* crazy. This is the third summer Joanie's worked here and she says that every summer Mr. Perry has to fire somebody. It's like an itch he can't control. She says he always fires somebody at least by the middle of the season and so far nobody's been fired. And do you know what else?"

"What else, for God's sake?"

"I think it's a toss-up between you and Mr. Gaston—as to who gets fired."

Stone raised up on one elbow, frowning. "Why Mr. Gaston?" He swung his feet to the floor. "Good God! People don't go around firing poor old guys eighty years old. That would be lousy."

"Yes, it would be."

"Hell, if it's a choice between me and Mr. Gaston, then I'd rather be the one."

"But then it would be on your record," Shirley said.

Stone shrugged. "Who gives a damn?"

Shirley looked sadly into his eyes. "You really *don't* give a damn, do you? About anything. For a little while you were okay. Now you're hiding in this damned horrible room again. Why, Jeff?"

"Because," he said. "I get tired and I have to lie down and rest."

Shirley shook her head. She picked up his hairbrush from

the orange crate. "Do you ever wash your hairbrush?"
"No."
"Would you like me to wash it for you?"
"No . . . thanks."
She replaced the hairbrush. "Are we friends?"
"Yes," he said. "We're friends."

Off-duty that afternoon, he walked northward. Up where
Ellen Hopper was staying, the beach narrowed so that between the boardwalk and the water there was barely room for
the line of bright umbrellas under which the guests reclined,
and when the tide came up it lapped at their feet, sending
them shrieking and scurrying.

In a black bathing suit, she sat alone beneath a black and
yellow umbrella, looking off to sea. Standing on the boardwalk, Stone saw a man approach her and kneel in the sand just
at the edge of the shadow cast by her umbrella. The man
talked with animation, grinning, showing his teeth, spreading
his hands, but Stone saw that she did not move and whatever
she said in reply caused the man to stop grinning, to run his
hand through his hair and leave.

She sat alone and looked off to sea, toward the small yellow
sailboat with the three tiny bronzed bodies perched on the
gunwale, running fast with the wind, paralleling the shore.

She sat alone, in the manner of one already spoken for,
already pledged.

Stone turned back, asking himself again why his father
had done it. How had he felt as the three of them sat there
on the patio? Perhaps he had felt nothing of depth. He had
merely been showing his mistress one of his possessions, with
some degree of pride, true, but with utterly no awareness of
the possession. His father was too late. Stone had grown older.
His father still thought of him as 14 or 15. At 14 or 15 Stone
might have accepted it without condemnation but now he was

old enough to condemn. He condemned his father for his insensitivity; for being so insensitive as to trot his son up the boardwalk to meet his mistress, the person he planned to marry if her letter could be believed. And he condemned him for his taste. Mrs. Hopper was coarse and stupid, she looked whorish. His mother was a person of refinement and breeding. His father had married and lived with one sort of woman. All along he had wanted another. The gravy boat finally was laughable. No wonder he couldn't tell the real reason.

* eleven

Among the help it was common knowledge that Mr. Perry felt Mr. Gaston was too old and feeble to keep things quiet at night, and probably not man enough even if he had been younger. Mr. Perry gave the impression that he was very angry that he had ever hired Mr. Gaston in the first place, except that he was not angry at himself for doing the hiring but at Mr. Gaston for being what he was.

Stone knew that the summer was a high point for the Gastons. At first they had seemed very happy. They had a married daughter, and Mrs. Gaston bragged about her daughter's husband, who was a scientist working for a large drug company which made vitamins and remedies for head colds. Mrs. Gaston told people he was well thought of by his company.

Over and over again, Mrs. Gaston had expressed her delight with her good fortune because after all, she asked, how often did people get a chance to spend the entire summer at the beach and get paid for it to boot.

At this point, having asked the rhetorical question, she would grow complacent. Her eyes would light up behind her rimless glasses and she would laugh a non-infectious laugh.

She loved Charlie and loved to have him kid her. One evening at supper Charlie told her to drop by the taproom sometimes and he'd buy her a shot. Mrs. Gaston went all to pieces laughing. Mr. Gaston smiled mildly and mildly ate his fried fish.

For the Gastons, things started going bad on the Fourth of July weekend, when people traditionally came to the beach to raise hell, drinking and making a lot of noise in their rooms, even though there were a lot of other people who wanted to get their sleep. On the Fourth of July weekend, Mr. Gaston was a total failure. Scattered through the hotel there were seven or eight pockets of hell-raisers and Mr. Gaston had been unable to do anything with them, even though he kept going upstairs and knocking on their doors and telling them they had to be quiet because there were other people trying to get their rest. The next morning Mr. Perry received plenty of complaints from those who had been trying to get their rest, and Shirley said that he then muttered and grumbled, demanding to know what he was paying Mr. Gaston for anyway, and complaining that Mr. Gaston obviously did not have the guts of a gazelle. All that day he told anybody who would listen that when Mr. Gaston tried to quiet the people down they all just laughed at him because he was too old and didn't have any guts. Mr. Perry seemed confident that when he got to be as old as Mr. Gaston he'd still have plenty of guts.

That evening at supper both the Gastons were very quiet and Stone concluded that Mr. Gaston must have caught hell from Mr. Perry.

When Mr. Gaston ate his pink junket, he seemed to eat it

furtively, with an attitude of guilt, and Stone wondered if Mr. Gaston felt he was undeserving of the junket because of not being a forceful enough person.

After finishing his junket, Mr. Gaston held his coffee cup in both hands, very carefully, and looked off into the distance with his coffee cup to his lips and then an inch or so away from his lips. His thick white hair was carefully combed as always. His neck was long and thin and his shirt collar too large.

That night, puzzled, at bay, Mr. Gaston told Mr. Perry that what they should do when people refused to keep quiet was to call the cops, but this only incensed Mr. Perry, who was already incensed, and happily working himself into a lather. He said this was absolutely unnecessary, that Mr. Gaston should be able to shut people up with the sheer force of his personality and that furthermore it would be an insult to his guests to threaten them with cops, and that calling the cops was *absolutely* forbidden.

Being the night clerk, Mr. Gaston slept all morning and part of the afternoon. About a week after the Fourth of July fiasco, he came down to the taproom as he sometimes did in late afternoon and ordered a beer. Taking a sip and smacking his lips, he asked Stone, "Have you had much contact with the *boss?*"

"No," Stone said. "Not very much."

"Well . . . you're lucky," Mr. Gaston said and chuckled, clearly hoping that Stone would join him, hoping to strike up a conversation in which they could both talk about what a lousy guy Mr. Perry was.

When Stone said nothing, Mr. Gaston looked toward the end of the bar, as though he felt he had a right to be angry and resentful but couldn't quite manage to look that way, and wondered why somebody didn't say something that would help him.

Stone tried to think of something but he couldn't think of anything very clever, so he said, "He's quite a character."

This was enough to please Mr. Gaston. "Quite a character!" he repeated happily. "He sure *is* quite a character, yessirree-*bob*, I'll tell the world he is. Some character is right, cap."

Drinking some more of his beer, he wiped his mouth on the cuff of his white shirt. He always wore a white shirt with long sleeves and a necktie.

"I wouldn't worry about it if I were you," Stone said. "Hey!"

"What's the trouble, boy?" Mr. Gaston asked.

"I've got an idea—if he gives you any more trouble, why don't you threaten to call the cops. Sic the *cops* on him."

Mr. Gaston's gnarled, liver-spotted fist came down hard on the bar. His eighty-year-old gums showed as he began to laugh, and his eyes grew watery.

Draining his beer, he seemed happy. "See you at supper, Jeff," he said.

"Yes sir," Stone said. "Maybe if we're lucky we'll have junket and fish."

Mr. Gaston went out laughing.

Stone smiled and then after a few seconds he looked gloomily at the bar.

During this period the cash was checking out okay, and from this it seemed almost a foregone conclusion that it would be Mr. Gaston who got fired. In Stone's view it was all Charlie's fault. If Charlie hadn't stopped lifting money from the cash drawer then it would have been Stone who got fired and Mr. Gaston's job as night clerk would have been secure. Mrs. Gaston would have continued to tell people how highly regarded her son-in-law was by the drug company for which he worked, something she no longer did.

On the night of July 12 there were some very rough customers in 206 and Mr. Gaston went about muttering to everybody except Mr. Perry that Mr. Perry should be more careful about some of the people he let into the hotel. There were two men in 206 and they had two girls in the room with them. All night long they kept sending down for more ice. After the bellboys went off duty, Mr. Gaston himself carried up a couple of pitchers of ice, asking them each time to please make less noise since people were trying to get their rest. One of them offered him a dime tip, which he declined, asking them again please to be quiet, and the other man told him, "Knock it off, Grandpa," and Mr. Gaston said all right, he was warning them for the last time.

Mr. Perry told Mr. Gaston that all he needed to handle people like this was a little fire in his makeup, and that if it happened again that night he was to wake up Mr. Perry and get him out of bed, if that's what it had come to.

So again that night the men in 206 started raising a lot of hell, and at three o'clock in the morning Mr. Gaston roused Mr. Perry.

Mr. Perry got out of bed and put on his bathrobe and slippers, but he did not go up to 206. Instead he went straight to the lobby and called the police, who came immediately and quieted things down.

Mr. Perry then told Mr. Gaston that he had frankly had about all he could take, and that Mr. Gaston was fired.

Shirley told Stone that Mr. Perry felt much better now that he had fired somebody.

Stone did not see the Gastons leave. He saw their feet leave, and he knew it was their feet because Shirley had told him they were leaving on the afternoon bus for Dover, Delaware, where they had lived all their lives.

After lunch he had gone to look for them to say goodbye

and to say something more if he could think of it, but they were not in their room, and he couldn't find them anywhere about the hotel.

But while he was on duty in the taproom he happened to look through one of the window slits near the ceiling, and through it he could see the sidewalk that people most likely would use in case they happened to be walking to the bus depot. Mr. Gaston's shoes were perforated and newly whitened for the bus trip. The cuffs and legs of his trousers were white with a faint black pinstripe. Near one foot was the bottom edge of a tan leather suitcase, and near the other foot was the bottom of a black suitcase.

Mr. Gaston's feet came first, and then came Mrs. Gaston's feet, and her shoes were black with thick low heels, the same kind of shoes that Lizzie wore, except that Mrs. Gaston's shoes were not mildewed so far as Stone could see. Swinging along near her right foot was an orange mesh shopping bag, and crammed into one of the bottom corners was a purple-blue jar of Noxzema.

Stone started to run after them and then he stood undecided behind the bar. The reason he stopped was that he had pictured the scene and didn't like it. He would raise his hand and call goodbye. They would turn and wave, and in the act of waving there would be a sort of humiliation for them, he felt sure of it, and he knew that his desire to wave goodbye was more for his own benefit than for theirs.

"So long, Mr. Gaston, you poor old bastard," he muttered, and then he did a few half-hearted clog steps, breaking off when he saw her come in, tensing up as she walked smiling to the bar. "Hello, Jeffrey," she said, holding out her hand. "I *told* you I'd drop by, and here I am . . ."

Stone looked into her eyes and they still looked like green ice. He took her hand briefly and dropped it. "Hello, Mrs. Hopper," he said.

* twelve

Having been raised in a strict code of politeness, Stone found that he was automatically polite in almost any circumstance. Even now he was reacting with reflexive politeness, taking comfort in the thought that politeness—icy politeness—was a weapon more potent than rudeness.

Mrs. Hopper was sitting on a barstool, clasping her slim, tanned hands on the bar and smiling at him. She had the air of a woman who had always done well with men, an air of total confidence in her own charm and sexuality; a woman who in fact had nothing beyond sexuality to offer but who had found it quite enough. Her light blue bathing suit was more or less concealed by a white cape-like garment which was fastened at the throat. Her face, instead of being one face, was two identical halves of a face, he thought, because of her hair being parted in the middle and because each eyebrow was brushed and tweezed with the same precision and her hair looped the same way behind each freshly tanned ear.

She was chattering about the atmosphere of the taproom and to Stone, searching earnestly for weaknesses, one weakness was her nose. Her nostrils, he told himself, were so vertical, so *confronting*, as to be almost piglike. Yet he knew that he was exaggerating out of the desire to exaggerate. It was simply that her nose was not the sort of nose Dolores del Rio had. Her nose merely was tilted in a way that some men, his father doubtless, might find fetching. Her legitimate weaknesses were her high-pitched voice, her truly horrible laugh, and the fact that she had said the other evening that somebody had given gasoline rationing stamps "to he and I." As Stone uncapped the coke she had ordered, and as he poured it carefully into a glass, he assured himself, clinging tight to the belief, that no woman could be attractive who used the nominative case where the accusative was so clearly called for.

She asked him if he had heard from his father and, wanting to say sardonically, "No, have you?", he said instead that he had not heard from him since he went back that night—or more probably the following morning, he wanted to say, after groveling about upon your ungrammatical loins. But all he said was, "No, not since he went back."

He reminded himself that she did not know he knew; that neither she nor his father knew that he had read the note in the pocket of his father's bathrobe. But this made no difference. Having her there before him made him twitch with discomfort, made him want to look down into corners, to study the contours of the half-empty coke bottle, the grain in the wood of the bar.

Sipping the coke thoughtfully, eyes dancing, she asked now, "Are you always so quiet as you were the other night, Jeffrey?"

Stone was standing with his back against the shelves that held the glasses, gripping the bar rag very tight in his right hand. "Was I quiet?" he asked.

"I should realize," she said, "that still water runs deep. Your father tells me you are a very bright boy."

"Really?" Stone asked.

"He's extremely proud of you," she said. "He says you've always been good at *everything*. Eagle Scout—were you really an Eagle Scout?"

Stone nodded.

"My younger brother always wanted so badly to get up to Eagle but he didn't make it. He got as far as, I think, Star?

Is it Star? And by then he was almost sixteen years old, so
he sort of lost interest."

Stone nodded.

"Your father says you were always president of your class
and always got such good grades. I think it's just wonderful,
I really do. I think it's wonderful for a boy to really try. So
now you're waiting to go into the army . . ."

"Yes," Stone said. "I am."

"How do you feel about it?"

"I'm not sure," Stone said.

"You know . . . when I was talking the other night about
gasoline rationing stamps, I didn't mean to give the impression
that I was one of those people who chisel and cheat . . . I
mean, as people go, I suppose I'm one of your old-fashioned
patriots. When I think of our poor boys on those merchant
ships getting blown up by German submaries and cast into the
sea . . . it just makes me boil, I mean it really does, I mean
Jeezy-Peezy."

Stone nodded.

"Well . . . tell me about yourself, Jeffrey."

"There's very little to tell," Stone said, happy that she had
used such an abominable expression as Jeezy-Peezy.

She smiled and began groping in her purse, handing him a
dollar. "Can you change this for me? I'm going to play a
record."

He gave her change from the cash register and watched as
she crossed the room to the juke box, and stood studying the
selection panel. The white cape had fallen away so that he
now saw once more the hard bulge of her breasts against the
sky-blue fabric of her bathing suit, the flat line of her stomach.
For a second or two, he was in bed with her, driving hard.

She was returning to the bar. "I played *Moonlight Serenade*
and *Little Brown Jug*," she said. "Is that all right with you? I
love Glenn Miller. My husband and I went to see him at the

Glen Island Casino last summer and he was simply marvelous. Do you like him?"

Stone nodded. "Pretty well."

"What's *your* favorite record?"

Stone looked at the coke bottle. "At the moment it's *Lester Leaps In*." .

"That's one I don't know. Who is it by?"

"Lester Young."

"I don't know him. Who is he?"

Stone was pleased at the disdain he felt. "He plays tenor saxophone for Basie."

"Oh," she said. "Yes. Some of your colored bands are terribly good, I *know*. But I go for the smoother kind, like Glenn Miller and Artie Shaw and Jan Savitt and of course Tommy Dorsey."

Stone nodded. She was making very little progress with her coke, and now she was humming *Little Brown Jug* along with the record. "Who else do you like, Jeffrey?"

Stone took a deep breath. "Shostakovitch."

"Who?"

"Shostakovitch."

"I don't know him."

Stone looked with contempt at her purse. "He's Russian. He writes classical music. Symphonies."

"Oh. I see. Well . . ." She laughed, and he winced as the sound waves assailed his ear. "I'll just stick with Glenn Miller if you don't mind."

Stone stood there trying to make up his mind whether to show off—trying to decide whether showing off would be a weakness or a strength, a capitulation or an asault. "The day is coming," he said, "when jazz and classical music are going to merge . . . come together."

"Really? And then what's going to happen?"

Stone looked deep into her green eyes, thinking that maybe what he was giving her was a sexy look. "Well . . ." he said, "Lester Young, for example, will start spilling his guts all through the orchestrations of, well, Shostakovitch for one."

"How interesting. Is that your theory?"

"It's what I'd like to see happen, that's all."

"That's interesting, Jeffrey, it really is . . . Your father tells me you are also quite a football player. Did you play in college?"

"Nope. I wasn't good enough. Just high school."

"Marvelous. That's just marvelous, Jeffrey. Well . . ." She looked at her glass, still almost full. "You don't mind if I don't quite finish this, do you?"

Stone shook his head.

"I should be getting back up the boardwalk, but it's been just wonderful talking with you. Come up and swim with me some time, Jeffrey. Teach me how to ride waves. The ocean positively terrifies me."

She gave him another smile and he thought, the bitch, she's fluttering her eyelashes at me, she's actually *fluttering her eyelashes* at me, oh my God.

He watched her walk out, watched the way she placed one foot on a line in front of the other, head high, shoulders back, walking in a way that reminded him of the way strippers walked.

✳ thirteen

Occasionally through the hole in the wall Stone could hear William muttering to himself. "Hmmmm," William would say. "Glass dropping," or "Hmmm, glass rising. Must be a front coming in."

When Stone asked him what he was talking about, William explained that he had a barometer in his room. He said it was a Christmas present from his mother and that he took daily readings and listed them in a notebook, which was a present from his brother. He said he also recorded the wind direction and approximate velocity, as well as whether it was sunny or cloudy, and if cloudy what kind of clouds. He said he felt that although weather forecasting was an inexact science it still paid better than being a bellhop and moreover did not involve carrying suitcases.

Stretched out on his cot, Stone nodded agreement. Presently he heard William go out.

Toward midnight Stone himself went out, walking idly southward. Even though it was late, people were strolling the boardwalk in couples and family groups, eating popcorn from pasteboard boxes. They walked slowly, expectantly, and their faces were neon-green. On a bench outside the dance hall, a sailor leaned over and vomited on his shoes. He straightened and wiped his mouth, then stood and spat hard with the wind. Wiping his mouth again, he slumped to the bench and closed his eyes.

Stone walked, feeling despair and finding despair in the

faces that passed. He asked himself if his despair was based in part on the thought that Ellen Hopper was more attractive physically than his mother, who was ladylike and young and pretty without being provocative. He felt this was how a mother should look. For a long moment he felt rage, felt the injustice of a mother being penalized for looking as a mother should look, for looking as it was fitting and becoming for a mother to look, to be penalized for looking like a lady instead of a whore.

Back in his room he lay still dressed on his cot, telling himself that he must do something, must detach himself from his stone-ness, because he was after all not a stone nor a window without a view, nor indeed an orange crate. He was a human being. As a human being he was not so clearly defined as a stone nor an orange crate. Certainly the stone and quite possibly the orange crate in some form would outlive him.

Lying there, he put into concrete thought something that he had merely sensed about himself, and this was his feeling about victims. He knew that so long as he lived he would always be on the side of the victims, and would never victimize; not out of a desire to be heroic or admirable but simply because of the sick revulsion he felt to witness a victim, to contemplate helplessness, to see a defenseless person over-powered, a horse beaten, a dog kicked.

For whatever reason, the faces of the people on the board-walk just now had had the look of victims. All the faces reminded him of the Gastons' faces and he thought again, as he had thought in the past few days, of the Gastons back home in Dover, Delaware, with time now for their lawn and flowers, with leisure to die. He saw Mr. Gaston alone at breakfast and wondered if Mr. Gaston had been able, at some point in his life, to discover as he himself had discovered that there was no essential difference between pain and pleasure,

that to a piece of machinery getting fired was no better, no
worse, than its opposite. He saw Mr. Gaston alone in the
kitchen, a piece of toast halfway to his lips, staring at the
kitchen wall at six o'clock in the morning and remembering
his moment of humiliation. He wondered if it was something
Mr. Gaston could handle. And he thought of Mr. Gaston
with his ear to the radio, listening to Gabriel Heatter and the
Lone Ranger, because Mr. Gaston had said these were his
favorite programs. Stone could imagine him listening, totally
absorbed, except for the sliver of self-doubt that remained and
gnawed at his manhood. Even a man of eighty would want to
respect his own manhood because to doubt it would be to cast
a shadow back over the whole eighty years; and although he
might listen intently to the radio there was a part of his
awareness that he could not give to listening because instead
of listening it would be suffering.

Stone knew that if he himself were heroic or even right-
thinking, he would refuse to work any longer for a bastard
like Mr. Perry, who was perhaps only part bastard, the rest
maniac. If he were truly to take the part of the victims, he
would quit, clear out, and he had considered it but rejected
it and he did not know for sure why. He could only conclude
that he hated the thought of returning home, but he also could
suspect that he stayed at the beach because it was where
Ellen Hopper was.

That evening before going to bed he wrote a letter to Mr.
Gaston telling him that he was badly missed and wishing him
a pleasant summer, autumn, winter and spring.

William had enlarged the hole in the wall, extending it
vertically and gouging it wider, using it as a mail slot. As a
favor to Stone and apparently because he himself got a kick
from it, William brought down Stone's infrequent mail and
dropped it through the hole, which was at a point just at the

foot of the bed, so that sometimes the letter fell to the floor and sometimes landed on the edge of the cot.

Stone awoke to find a letter from his father. The letter ignored what had passed between them. It said that his father had enjoyed seeing him and had returned to heat and more heat, and then discussed the inaccuracy with which the weather bureau was able to predict thunderstorms which might have cooled the air even if only temporarily, concluding that a brief respite from heat was better than no respite at all. The letter also mentioned a Gallup Poll indicating that the populace was overwhelmingly opposed to U.S. entry into the war.

That night after locking up the taproom, Stone went to his cot but found that he could neither read nor sleep, so he went back to the taproom, unlocking it but not turning on the light.

He pulled up a stool and sat in the dark with his head down on the bar, thinking of all the things it gave him pain to think about.

Presently he heard footsteps moving along the passageway toward his room and then returning. "Jeff . . ." Shirley was moving into the storeroom, pausing. "Are you in there?"

"Yeah." he answered.

"I saw the door open. . . . What the hell . . ." She was groping about in the dark, touching his shoulder. "Is anything wrong?

"No."

"Can I sit with you? As a friend?"

"Sure, if you want to."

"I'll be very quiet."

"You don't have to. What have you been doing?"

"I've been thinking," Shirley said.

"Is that all?"

"I've been thinking that so much of whether a girl is a good person depends on whether her husband is a good person, wouldn't you say that?"

"I guess so."

"I've been reading about people who are forces for good. I think that when I get older I'll be able to be a force for good."

"Whatever that is," Stone said.

"I'll know what it is when the time comes," Shirley said.

In the darkness he reached for her hand, running his knuckles lightly over her wrist. "I think you probably will," he said.

"I couldn't *possibly* have been anything as young as I was, with the husband I had," she said.

"Did your husband get a job after the baby was born?" Stone asked.

"Yes, he got a job in a shoe store. It was the worst shoe store in Scranton, Pennsylvania. He said he was going to night school so he could get his high school diploma but the shoe store didn't close until nine at night, so he didn't."

"You mean you were ahead of him in school?"

"A year ahead. I graduated but he didn't."

"Yeah." Stone said, "I remember. You were Class Historian because of the way you were built."

"That's right. I'm sure it was the first time in the history of our high school that a graduating class had a Class Historian who was pregnant. I can't be sure, of course."

"Of course," Stone said.

"Laugh, Stone."

"Why?"

"I don't know. I just like it when you laugh. Can I play a record?"

"God, no. Mr. Perry will come thumping down here and raise hell."

"It's depressing down here," she said. "Let's get out."

"Where?"

"I don't know. Up on the boardwalk."

They sat on the edge of the boardwalk in front of the hotel and Shirley said, "I thought you were going to find me a husband."

"I'm looking," Stone said. "Every day I go out on the boardwalk and look up and down."

"Like hell you do." She laughed. "No kidding, Stone."

"No kidding what?"

"I don't know. At first when you said you'd help me find a husband it hurt me. I couldn't take it. But now I can. Now I'm not hurt by hearing you say it. Except, damn it, you're not helping me."

"How in the hell can *I* help you?"

"Laugh, Stone."

"Ha ha," Stone said.

"Very good. . . . I don't know. You could help me by making me smarter, so I could find a smart husband."

"You're already smart."

"Oh, the hell I am. Listen, you've been to *college* for God's sake. Teach me some of the things you learned. If you told me a few smart-ass things to say, then I could impress some rich guy out on the beach. Okay?"

Stone laughed.

"Hey, you laughed, Stone. And it wasn't just ha-ha."

"I know. I apologize."

"Oh, God!" Shirley said. "That really sums you up. What you just said. You feel *guilty* if you laugh, don't you, Stone? No kidding, Stone, come on. Teach me some things. If you're not going to screw me you can at least *teach* me."

"Teach you *what?*"

"Whatever you learned in college. Teach me."

"What I learned wouldn't do you any good."

"Hell, you must have learned *something*. You were there four years, weren't you? *Okay* then."

Stone said nothing. He picked up her hand from where it lay on the boardwalk and held her wrist on his lap.

"Hey, watch it, Stone, you're getting pretty sexy there, be careful."

He returned her hand to the boardwalk and sat in silence, looking out over the dark ocean.

"Have you thought of anything else," Shirley asked.

"I'm thinking of something else," he said. "You know what's sort of a surprise to me? I guess I'm naive."

"Well I *know* that," Shirley said. "In what way?"

"I guess what I can't get used to is the idea that when people get old, I mean when they get up in their *forties*, even, they still go to bed with each other."

Shirley yelped with laughter. "Are you kidding, you damned fool? Of *course* they do. Hell, my grandfather was the town stud when he was in his *sixties*. He was as bad as Charlie. Oh my God, Stone, you really are a stupid dumb bastard."

"I guess I am," Stone said.

Stone confirmed to himself that Mrs. Hopper found walking important. He watched her trying to walk from the hips, trying to make the weight of each step disappear somewhere before her foot touched the ground. He saw her coming along the boardwalk at twilight, wearing her dark glasses and holding her shoulders back, walking very lightly, as if she had been twice taught to walk, once as an infant and again later in life. Now she saw him and began to smile, walking a little faster and taking off her dark glasses and shaking out her long black hair, which this evening had no center part, and this, he felt, made her look even more like a stripper. "*Hello,*

Jeffrey," she said. "How nice to see you. What are you doing up at this end of the boardwalk? Did you come up to see me —I hope?"

Stone looked at her gravely. "Why do you hope?"

"Because I'd be flattered."

"I was just out taking a walk," he said.

"Can I invite you up to *our* taproom and buy *you* a coke?"

"No thanks," he said. "I have to get back."

"Or for that matter, a drink? Do you drink?"

Stone nodded. "Sometimes. But I can't now."

She looked at him curiously and then looked over the sea, narrowing he eyes, watching a plane, a blue and silver bullet, growing large against the limpid evening sky. "You're an interesting boy, Jeffrey," she said softly.

Stone looked down at her slim tanned legs, at her thong sandals. "In what way?"

She patted his shoulder. Once more she was maternal. "I just think you are. Shouldn't that plane have its lights on?"

Stone looked at the plane. "I guess it should."

"Don't forget," she said. "You were going to teach me how to ride waves. Don't forget now."

"Okay, good night," Stone said.

"Good night, Jeffrey."

Half a block away, he turned and looked back. She was still standing at the edge of the boardwalk, looking after him. He walked on through the fading light.

* fourteen

Lizzie was sick for a while and Stone went to see her in her room, which was also in the basement although it had a real window, one which looked out upon the alley and hence commanded a view of overflowing garbage cans and of the clothesline where the guests' swimming attire was hung to dry. Her room was the size of Stone's but seemed larger because it had no pillar. Lizzie's black shoes were placed on the windowsill where the late afternoon sun was making a direct attack on the mildew that coated the eyelets. On one wall there was a calendar with a naked white woman bending forward to kiss an apple blossom.

Stone, pausing just inside the door, asked her how she felt.

Lizzie lay on her cot, glowering. Her pillow she had placed on her chest as a matter of modesty. Blinking rapidly, she said she felt terrible, that she had felt terrible all summer, and that she was sure she wouldn't be feeling this way if she were still upstairs performing her duties as chambermaid. She said that in her days as a chambermaid many of the guests would ask year after year for rooms on her floor because they liked her so much and didn't want any other chambermaid.

"They still do now," she said. "They come in with their grip and ask William where Lizzie and he tell where I am, down that durn bathhouse."

Stone asked her about the doctor and she said a doctor had been there, had given her some medicine and told her she could get up the following day. He asked her what was wrong exactly, and she said she had some "durn pains."

Stone left her with the blanket pulled up to her chin,

clasping the pillow to her chest, swaddled with rage that she was no longer young enough to be a chambermaid.

The next day she was up and around, performing her bath-house and cooking duties as usual. At lunch she asked Stone if he had a car. "No," he said. "Why?"

She said she had to go inland to get something from her house and needed somebody to drive her over. Stone said he would borrow Charlie's car and take her over after supper.

That evening, after Lizzie had finished up in the kitchen, Stone picked her up at the alley entrance and they set out, Lizzie sitting next to him in the front seat.

Driving over the bridge that crossed the back bay, Stone realized that it was the first time he had left the resort since his arrival in early June. In the rear view mirror, he could see the hotels and cottages, glittering white in the slanted light of the falling sun. He told Lizzie to turn and look because it was a sight worth seeing. Lizzie didn't turn. She just nodded and said, "Pretty place," as if it was something she took for granted.

Their destination was a small town about seven miles inland and Lizzie gave him directions. As they entered the town and passed a cemetery, she said, "There's the white folks grave yard, ain't it pretty? Ours a mess."

She began batting her eyes and scowling up at the con-vertible top then scowled at Stone. Ahead there was a cluster of unpainted, sloping houses and a store with a huge Coca Cola sign covering one whole side. "Slow down," Lizzie said. Then she demanded, "Listen, boy, ain't this one of them kind of cars? *You* know, Gawd durn it. Where the top to it comes down? Well then, Gawd's sake, put it down, boy, put it *down*." Lizzie scowled. She snatched angrily at the collar of her black cloth coat.

Stone stopped the car, got out and lowered the top, pounding and patting it into place. Lizzie smiled. Stone started off again, and Lizzie scowled. "Drive *slower*, Gawd durn it, slow this thing *down*."

People appeared at the side of the dusty road, moved to the front edge of their sloping porches, smiling and waving. "Drive slower, drive *slower*, bet I'll hit you directly, Jeff," Lizzie muttered. "That's it, that's it. That's a good boy."

The sun now was down and there was a mellow, dust-filled lavender light falling upon the road and upon the sloping houses. Lizzie waved, looking from side to side, laughing, nodding, simpering. The breeze tickled the white wisps of her hair, showing patches of brown scalp. "How do," she said, nodding to her friends on their porches. "How do," she said over and over again. "How do. It's Lizzie." At times she merely shaped the words with her lips, whispering, "How do, it's Lizzie."

The road stopped before it reached her house, brought up short by an overgrown field. Lizzie told him to stop. "You stay right here," she said, and set out across the field, following an invisible path, wading through weeds that sprang up again in her wake. Stone looked at the house. It looked not unlike Lizzie. It was top-heavy, a cumbersome, unpainted, two-story shaft of a house, softened by the lavender twilight, careening dangerously above a sea of weeds.

It was nearly dark when Lizzie came out. Stone did not hear the front door close, but then he saw her wading through the weeds toward the car. She got in, holding in her lap a flat, oblong object, wrapped in brown paper and tied with a string. "This the Lord Jesus," she explained. "His picture."

"Is that what you came to get?" Stone asked.

For a few moments she didn't answer. Then she said, "I wanted to see that durn house."

"That's where you live in the winter?" Stone asked.

"Gawd yes."

Stone backed the car around and started off again but she stopped him and told him to put up the top because she was getting chilly and it was nearly dark.

On the drive back she told him she hated the house in the field and hated the winters when the hotel closed, because she hated living alone in the field and hated the way Mr. Perry ran the hotel.

"Any hotel with good sense would stay open all year round," she said.

She told him that she was very afraid, not so much of dying but of being alone when she died.

"Think I get me one of them birds," she said. "You know, one of them pollies. Teach him to talk. Say, 'goodbye, Lizzie, goodbye, old girl, you been a good old girl.' In case when I die there's nobody around to say goodbye."

She asked him how long it would take to teach a parrot to talk.

"I'm not sure," Stone said. "Maybe not so very long."

"I treat him nice," Lizzie said. "Buy him seed to eat."

When they got back to the hotel, she told him to go find a hammer and a nail, and then directed him while he hung the picture of the Lord Jesus on the wall, next to the picture of the naked white woman who was bending forward to kiss the apple blossom.

Taking Lizzie home made Stone feel good. He also felt sad but he rather liked the combination of goodness and sadness that he felt. It seemed somehow to induce serenity and hope, a feeling of calm. After returning Charlie's car keys, he went into his room and propped himself up in bed with a pad of lined paper and his fountain pen.

For five minutes or so, he stared at the pad, jabbing it softly with the fountain pen, making many small dots, and then he wrote:

Dear Dad,

   I realize I'm probably too young to feel what you're feeling and too young to understand all the reasons you have for doing what you're doing. But I'm writing to make another attempt to convince you, even though I don't really know how to go about it. I'd just like to say that I think you're making a very big mistake and one you'll come to regret. It seems to me that if you cut mother out of your life you'll be cutting out a large part of yourself because you'll be renouncing and sort of demeaning all the years that were a certain you and that were us. And so it seems to me that you'd be renouncing twenty years of yourself. I should think that would make you feel pretty lousy in any new life, knowing you had left such a big chunk of yourself behind. I happen to think mother is a very good person and one who doesn't deserve to be made a victim. I keep wondering what happened between the two of you and I'm wondering if it might be something so simple as the fact that too much of your life together has been spent working. Sometimes I think that both of you have worked so hard and concentrated so much on the three of us that you haven't had much time for each other. Maybe that's part of the trouble.

   Anyway I've come up with an idea and I hope you'll do it. I've got no idea when I'm going to be called up for induction. For all I know it may not be until November. Anyway, here's what I'd like to offer. This place closes right after Labor Day and I'll come right home and hold down the house, look after Robbie and Tom, while you and mother go off somewhere on a vacation, just the two of you. Or if you'd rather, I'll quit this job right now and come home so you can do it now if you'd rather. And I'd like to treat the two of you. I've saved some money from this job, mainly because I don't spend any to speak of, and I've already saved up $65 which you can use. Go some place decent, maybe Atlantic City or

Stone found that he was now staring into space, the fountain pen poised an inch or so above the lined pad. William was playing his radio and although it was not on very loud Stone could hear it and he found himself listening to a skit featuring Hollywood actors who were famous for playing gangster roles. The skit illustrated what a good buy defense bonds were. The actors, in a tough, gangster way, held up a man and stole his defense bond, only to find that it had availed them nothing since the defense bond could only be cashed by its rightful owner. Stone had been given a one hundred dollar defense bond by his mother and father for his twenty-first birthday.

He finished the letter:

> Massachusetts or some place like that. I hope you'll do it. Let me know. It would mean a great deal to me. Love, Jeff.

He folded the letter and put it into an envelope, then addressed it to his father's office. For a while he lay there looking at it as if it were something rather precious, an object of treasure. Finally he went out and dropped it into the mailbox that stood on the boardwalk just outside the hotel, jiggling the lid a few times to make sure the letter went down.

* fifteen

It seemed, Stone thought, a very long time since he had felt young, yet it had been only four months ago. Then, in the early weeks of his final semester, he had been absorbed with his own pursuits, sometimes getting drunk on weekends, inhabiting blue-smoke cellar clubs where jazz music was purveyed, doing a term paper on Thorstein Veblen. The war was a grim reality but one far in the future and one which might never affect him because Roosevelt after all had promised to keep the United States out of it. Of far more immediate personal importance were Basie's latest recordings, Veblen's feelings about conspicuous consumption.

He could not have said for certain why he now began to feel young again, but he thought it was because of the letter he had written his father and because of the letter he felt might now come in reply. He waited for the letter to drop through the slot in the wall, hit his cot and fall to the floor, and in his sleep he would hear it and bound up from his cot.

It was possible, of course, that he was being naive, that in reply his father would write of thunderstorms and summer heat, yet this time somehow he thought not. He and his father after all were of the same blood and marrow and something he felt so strongly about could not fail to be felt by his father. He didn't see how his father could very well refuse his offer, particularly when he had said right in the letter how much it meant to him.

So he waited, feeling hope and feeling young, and while he waited, in his off-duty hours, he swam in the ocean and lay in the sun and one afternoon took part in a touch football game. Sprinting in the damp, hard-packed sand to catch a long pass, he felt that his feet and legs had a spring and lightness they had not had all summer long. Shirley was watching him and he was aware that she was watching him and he was aware of wanting her to admire what she saw. Once he plucked the ball from the air just as it was about to hit her in the head. In the process he kicked sand all over her blanket, and she yelled, "Hey, you stupid dumb bastard, watch out." Laughing, he patted her head and trotted back to the game.

During this period he was spending a great deal of time with Shirley and finding it a pleasure. Although at first he had thought she was joking, he found she was at least half serious about learning from him, and although he laughed at her, and at the notion that he had anything to teach, she kept pressing. On a night when they sat again in the taproom after hours, she said, "Come on, Jeff, seriously, tell me what you learned in college. I really want to know."

"I told you," he said. "I didn't learn anything."

"Come on, Jeff."

"Well . . . okay, I learned how to form a corporation, in case you're planning to form a corporation."

"What else?"

"I learned the principles of accounting. How to do a balance sheet and a profit and loss statement."

"Hell . . . ," Shirley began to laugh. "You really *didn't* learn very much, did you?"

"I learned a few other things."

"What really got *to* you? What did you really *like?* I mean, in high school I took one year of Latin and flunked it but the teacher told us about how the Romans built their roads and I really liked that."

"Yeah," Stone said. "They built good roads."

"They sure must have."

"Why did you flunk Latin?"

"I don't know. I think I was too busy being a sexpot and getting myself knocked up. But I was never really dumb, no kidding, I really wasn't, Stone. I just flunked things, that's all."

"Oh," Stone said.

She reached for his arm in the dark and hit it hard with her fist. "What else did you learn?"

"Well, I took a philosophy course I liked."

"Tell me about that."

"Well, for example, how do we know this is a taproom and how do we know it's dark in here?"

"Go to hell, Stone."

"I'm serious."

"Well I'm serious too. Go to hell, if that's what you learned in college."

"For that matter, how do we even know we're here?"

"Where?"

"Here, in the taproom."

"Go to hell, Stone."

"Okay, the hell with it then."

"Listen," Shirley said, "I'm *here*. That's something I really know. I'm here. I-AM-*HERE*."

"You think you are, that's all. Okay, let's take this bar. No. Let's take a window instead. I'll bet you think it's okay to speak of windows, don't you? You probably do."

"Go screw yourself, Stone."

"Okay. But *actually* it's wrong to speak of windows."

"It is?"

"We tend to categorize. Actually there is no such thing as *windows*. There is this window and that window, you know —Window A and Window A-Prime and Window B-Prime and so forth, on up to infinity."

"You mean that's the real way to look at windows?"

"Yes."

"How much was the tuition where you went?"

Stone laughed.

"So what else?" Shirley asked.

"Heidegger."

"Who in the hell is he?"

"A German philosopher. He said that reason . . . rationalism . . . what we call logic . . . is not all that important. That there are some things we know in our guts, even though we can't prove them."

"I'm on his side," Shirley said. "I know in my guts that I'm here in the taproom in the dark, even though I can't prove it. I mean, *you* may think you're up on the sand dunes getting laid, but I know damn well where *I* am. Right here in the taproom."

"Okay." Stone laughed and patted her head.

"Didn't you learn anything practical?" she asked.

"Yeah, I already told you. How to form a corporation."

The next morning she saw him on the boardwalk. Pointing to the front of the hotel, she said, "See those things with glass, Stone? They look like windows, which is a damn fool way of looking at it because we all know they are *not* windows, right?"

Stone laughed. "You're getting it."

"And as for you, Stone, you look like somebody smart but actually you're a dumb bastard."

"Right," Stone said. "I am."

He turned and watched her run up the front steps of the hotel into the lobby. The tan of her legs exactly matched the shade of her khaki skirt.

She was opening the screen door again and yelling, "Will you be on the beach this afternoon?"

Stone nodded.

In the afternoon he lay on her blanket, looking straight up at a sky of enormous purity, an empty sky except for a red box-kite sailing high against the deep moist blue, straining against its kite string, bobbing and tumbling and then righting itself and stretching the string taut in the steady breeze.

He wore only his swimming trunks and the sun felt good against his bare chest and legs. He could smell its heat and it struck him as strange that warmth could have a smell. He inhaled the warmth and the salt air, raising his chest high and letting it drop. All about him he could hear the cries of pleasure, at many levels of distance and volume and pitch, a cantata of pleasure against the dull thunder of the surf.

"How about some cultural things?" Shirley was lying with her head just behind his head, and her body sprawled at right angles to his. Looking straight up at the sky, watching the kite, he could not see her.

"What do you mean, cultural things? "he asked.

"Hell, I don't know. Cultural things."

"You mean like art? Okay, I took a one-semester art appreciation course. I know about the Dutch School."

"The *hell* you do! . . . What Dutch school?"

"Dutch painters. This guy you're going to meet, you could ask him what he thinks of the Dutch School. Then you could throw a few things at him. You can say you feel that Rembrandt is somber and that Pieter de Hooch . . ."

"*Who?*"

"Pieter de Hooch. He's one. Say you think Pieter de Hooch is nice but much too photographic."

"Pieter de Hooch is much too photographic." Shirley laughed. "You mean—too lifelike?"

"Right."

"Okay." Shirley shifted her body around so that she faced him. "Pieter de Hooch is nice . . ." She shrugged. "But frankly for my taste, he's much too photographic. He used a camera instead of a paint brush."

"Or would have if cameras had been invented. Hey, that's good, Shirley."

"Or would have if cameras had been invented," Shirley said. "Hey! I've got it, Jeff, a very good line. Now take Pieter de Hooch. As a painter, the son of a bitch would have made a good photographer."

Stone laughed. "Good."

"Suppose he never heard of Pieter de Hooch?"

"So much the better. Then he feels inferior because you have and he hasn't."

"Who does?"

"This guy you're going to meet . . . whoever he is."

"Hey, Stone," she said softly. "You really are a smart-ass. No kidding. Hey, Stone. . . . See that guy down there, the bald-headed guy under the green umbrella. I'm going to try it out on him."

"Do you think that would be a nice thing to do?"

"Why not?" Shirley got to her feet and brushed the sand from her legs. "I'm going to start out by throwing that one at him about how do we know we're sitting here on the beach for *sure* . . ." She grinned down at Stone. "Okay?"

"I can't stop you."

He watched as she walked down to the water, lithe, tanned and blonde in her pink gingham bathing suit, skin the shade of honey, a honey-blonde, he thought, watching as she moved along the wet sand as if she were simply taking a walk.

When she reached a point abreast of the green umbrella, she paused and looked toward the boardwalk, frowning, then moved up the incline of softer dry sand and knelt on one knee, smiling. Stone saw the man take a wrist watch from the pocket of a beach jacket and show it to her. Shirley nodded and smiled and then got down on both knees, still smiling. She nodded. The man grinned and ran a hand over his bald head. Shirley sat in the sand, drawing up her legs and pouring a fistful of sand over one ankle. She shrugged and spread her hands, then grabbed up more sand and poured it over her legs, looking somberly at the sand she was pouring. Then her face brightened and moved one hand through the air as if she were pointing to a beachscape, a seascape, and then said something, raising her eyebrows. She shook her head emphatically and poured more sand over her legs. Then, smiling, she got to her feet. The man got to his feet. She held out her hand and the man grasped it, nodding and grinning. Shirley walked away, turned once, waved, and then kept going down to the water's edge and headed southward for a couple of hundred yards, then circled back to the boardwalk and disappeared into the hotel.

Another time they walked far up the beach all the way to the dunes in late afternoon. "What do you think of the way I talk, Jeff? Do I talk like I came from the coal mines?"

"I don't know how people talk in the coal mines," Stone said.

"Well, I don't talk like *you* do, for instance. You're refined."

"Hell, I'm not all that refined."

"You give a good impression. You make people think you are."

"I can turn it on when I feel like it," he said.

"I've heard you with that phony refined voice, saying things like, 'yes, it looks as though it were . . .' And I hate your guts for it, Stone."

"What would *you* say?"

"I'd say, it looks like it is."

"Well, actually that's not right grammatically, Shirley, not that I give a damn. But just for the sake of argument, after a verb like *looks* or *acts* or *seems* or something like that, you put *as if*, or *as though* and you say *were* because its the sub-junctive. For example, you use *were* if it's not actually true."

"What the hell does all that mean?"

"Okay. Let's say, he looks as though he were bowling. Actually he's not bowling. He just looks like—I mean looks as if he were."

Shirley walked for a while in silence. "She looks as though she were getting laid, although actually she is not. Is that the way it works, Jeff?"

"That's pretty much the way it works, Shirley."

"Bastard."

"You're smart, Shirley."

"Do you really think so?"

"I really do. No kidding."

"Gosh . . ."

"Don't ever fall for any of this crazy stuff about feeling inferior, just because you only finished high school."

"Do you know something, Jeff? You've given me con-fidence."

"You're going to be a terrific person, Shirley. You already are."

She laughed. "I caught that old bastard Perry yesterday. I spelled 'accommodation' with two m's and he said there was only one m and I showed him the word in the dictionary and there were two. All these years that dumb bastard has been spelling accommodation with one m. I'm smart, Stone. I really am *smart*. No *kidding*."

She grabbed a handful of sand and flung it into the air, watching it drift with the wind.

"No kidding," Stone said. "You really are."

"I really *am*." Shirley pirouetted and started running and leaping.

They sat on the beach and he told her his theory about pain and pleasure, describing the panic he had felt on the night of his sunburn.

Shirley listened carefully, scoffing and occasonally frowning. As they were walking back, she said, "I can say the same thing to myself then. I can say there's no real difference between getting screwed and *not* getting screwed, right? That's what I'm saying to myself right now."

"God, Shirley, you've really got a one-track mind. Don't you ever think of anything else?"

"Sometimes." He put his arm about her waist as they walked and she pulled his hand around to the warmth of her stomach. "Why not, Stone?"

"Because you might get too attached to me," he said. "Just let me alone and go find a husband."

"Conceited dumb bastard."

"No I'm not. I'm just trying to be decent, for God's sake."

"Is the reason you won't screw me because you're afraid of knocking me up?"

"No."

"Then why?"

"Because you're an ugly bitch," he said.

Stone took her to the movies and the newsreel showed a Russian family getting a medal which had been awarded after death to a son who had stuffed a grenade down the turret of a German tank, blowing it up. But then, running for cover, the boy had been wiped out by a machine-gun.

Holding Shirley's hand, Stone looked intently at the screen, at the Russian family, the father and mother and three younger brothers. Their faces showed grief but also pride. Their faces made him think of wheat fields and cold Russian sunlight. A Russian general with a lot of medals on his chest then pinned a medal on the ill-fitting dress of the Russian mother and stepped back, bowing very low.

Stone thought of his own brothers, with their skinny,

bronzed rib-cages, going every day to the public pool. If he got killed in the war, he thought, it would be better to know that his family was proud and intact, like the Russian family. It would be better to know that his father and mother and two brothers were all sitting together around the dining room table, contentedly ladling gravy from the new gravy boat with plate attached.

"Will you buy me a snowball, Jeff?"

Stone stopped walking. He turned to Shirley and nodded, feeling dazed. By now they had left the movie house and were half way back to the hotel, passing the concession stands that lined the boardwalk. Stone had no recollection of getting there, no recollection of leaving the movie house.

Taking Shirley's hand, he drew her back to the snowball stand. "She'd like a snowball," he explained to the man behind the counter.

"What flavor?" the man asked.

In the garish purple neon light, Shirley was smiling and although she answered the man she was looking at Stone. "Lime," she said.

As they walked on back toward the hotel, he watched her spoon up the green ice and watched her eyes light up when she looked at him. "I figured out something," she said. "Something pretty smart."

"What?"

"Okay, Hitler is a German, right? And he reads all those German philosophers. So he figured out to himself that all those poor Jews he killed in concentration camps didn't really exist, and that if they did exist they didn't really know the difference because there is no difference between pain and pleasure anyway, right?"

Stone didn't answer. He walked beside her, glancing toward the ocean, seeing the white foam of the marching breakers.

"Stone . . ."

"Who knows?" he said. "Maybe that's exactly what he *did* tell himself."

"Which makes him a stark raving mad maniac bastard, right?"

"Right," Stone said.

"So there would be no limit to what people could do and couldn't do, right?"

"Right."

"Which means that somebody has got to go over there and kill the bastard, right?"

"Right," Stone said. "Right, Shirl."

"You called me Shirl."

"Yeah. I called you Shirl."

∗ sixteen

As the new night clerk, Mr. Perry hired a part-time preacher named Bob Parker, but only after a long period of search during which Mr. Perry himself had to sit up in the lobby six nights in a row.

The Reverend Parker was assigned to the downstairs help's dining room, and Stone met him at supper a few nights after his arrival, finding him sharp of feature, surprisingly young, certainly no more than thirty, and possessed of a truly remarkable voice, deep and rich and all over the scale, a powerful, perfectly controlled instrument of which he seemed very proud.

As Parker spooned up his pink junket, he told Stone that he had a circuit of country churches at which he preached on Sundays during nine months of the year. His summers were free and he said he used them in various ways, telling Stone with an engaging grin that the work of the Lord had many guises.

"Many, many guises," he thundered, causing Lizzie to turn from the sink, eyes popping at the sheer resonance and volume of his voice.

Parker took out a pipe and filled it with sweet-smelling tobacco. He wore a white knit sports shirt and khaki pants, and as he leaned back in his chair, drawing on the pipe, it was impossible to escape the impression that he was determined to be a regular fellow, one of the guys—man-of-the-cloth though he might be.

His eyes were russet, nearly matching his russet eyebrows and russet hair. "And you, Jeff," he said. "Tell me about *you.* Are you a college student?"

"I just graduated," Stone said.

"And how do we stand in the draft?"

"I'm waiting to go," Stone said.

Lizzie was listening with fascinaton. Parker apparently had set something in motion deep in her being, whether because of his enormous voice or because she was aware of being in the presence of the clergy. Stone had the fleeting impression that she was about to start clapping and chanting.

"Hmmmm, waiting to go, eh?" Parker said. "And how do we *feel* about the draft?"

Stone shrugged. "It's inevitable, I guess."

Parker's eyes bored into his. He nodded, drawing at his pipe, and kept looking into Stone's eyes until Stone began to feel uncomfortable and looked away. He had the feeling that Parker had deliberately looked him in the eye as a demonstration of his ability to look people in the eye.

"Well . . ." Parker said in a low, rich voice," "as I said before . . ." And now his voice rose and grew even richer. "Many, many guises."

"Amen," Lizzie said.

The next afternoon Parker came down to the taproom while Shirley was sitting at the bar in her pink gingham bathing suit. Stone introduced them and Parker told Shirley about his circuit of country churches. Shirley asked him how he worked it exactly, and he said that each Sunday he preached the same sermon at the four churches on his circuit and then, the following Sunday, preached a new one. Shirley asked him how he went about it and he said he usually took a text from the Bible—

"Oh!" Shirley squealed. "The *Bible!*"

Parker looked amused. "Yes," he said. "Of *course*, the Bible. I take a text from the Bible and embroider it, you see, into a feature length sermon."

At this point his eyes fell upon the front of Shirley's bathing suit and he quickly removed them, although not quite so quickly, Stone thought, as he might have.

Shirley said, "Suppose some people in one church decide to go to another church the same Sunday. Then they'd be hearing the same sermon twice, wouldn't they?"

Parker said it was the chance they took, that if they chose to go to church twice in one day it was their affair, not his.

Shirley hauled up the front of her bathing suit and asked him how he felt about the Bible.

"How do I feel about the Bible?" Parker smiled indulgently and re-lit his pipe. "Well, let's just say I like it, shall we?"

"Gosh yes," Shirley said. "I've been reading the Bible myself a great deal lately, and there is one thing that has occurred to me. It's as though it were . . ." She looked at Stone. ". . . as if it were . . . as though it were—well, I mean, how can we be absolutely certain that what we're reading really *is* the Bible?"

"Hmmm," Parker said with interest. His eyes now bored into Shirley's. He was standing beside her and Shirley, seated on a barstool, looked up at him, meeting his gaze, blinking a little. "May I judge . . ." Parker thundered, and then lowered his voice, "that you were about to go out on the beach?" Shirley smiled and nodded. "May I join you?"

As they walked from the taproom, Shirley looked back over her shoulder at Stone, briefly letting her mouth fall open and crossing her eyes.

The next day Shirley told Stone that Parker, in addition to preaching, had done a great deal of acting with amateur theatrical groups and had in fact once played the soldier in *Voice of the Turtle*, as well as the Boris Karloff part in *Arsenic and Old Lace*. He also took part in church benefits and was an accomplished acrobat and juggler.

"Maybe he's the guy you've been looking for," Stone said.

"Are you kidding? He's got the sex appeal of a sand crab."

"Did you try him out on Pieter de Hooch?"

"No. Seriously, Jeff, he's very interesting."

"In what way?"

"He has enormous ambition. He really wants to be a famous preacher some day, I mean sort of a national figure, and he feels that all this acting experience is something he'll be able to use, because he thinks a preacher has to be something of an actor and entertainer and medicine man and con-man. I mean he's very frank about it."

Stone, to his surprise, found that he was faintly jealous of Shirley's interest in Parker, and he took another look. For a man with such a powerful voice, Parker's shoulders were quite narrow and he had no breadth of chest. His face was hardly good looking, although on the other hand not bad looking. It was lean and chiseled, with a very sharp jawline and a long pointed nose. His russet hair was cleanly parted and slicked down so smooth as to make his nose and other features even more prominent. Stone found himself rather pleased that Shirley felt Parker had the sex appeal of a sand crab.

Yet Parker's arrival, along with his father's continued silence, seemed now to combine to break the brief mood of hope that he had felt in the sun-drenched, light and airy days with Shirley. The only letter that dropped through the slot in the wall was from his mother saying that his father was enormously busy. She also said that when she had gone to the hardware store to buy some bug spray for her rosebushes, the hardware man had expressed the firm conviction that the United States would not enter the war. She said that every night she prayed that this would be the case.

In the newspaper Stone read that as of mid-summer of 1941, army morale was alarmingly low. A noted psychiatrist, commenting upon different attitudes toward army enlistment, said that it was "an unsettled question whether enlistment should be considered primarily an opportunity for expressing unrepressed belligerency and brutality in a good cause; a chance to get vocational training; an unpleasant patriotic obligation to be evaded as honorably as possible; a course of discipline and treatment for reckless, wayward, spineless, maladjusted young male adults, or a course of punishment for recalcitrant individuals in need of a firm hand."

He wondered which of these applied to himself and decided that none did.

Sometimes Stone, without intending to, found that he was eating supper with Parker, just the two of them, while Lizzie stood by at the sink or the stove.

One evening Lizzie said that Parker, being a preacher, should know what heaven was like, and she asked him to describe it.

"Do you mean physically?" Parker intoned.

Lizzie cocked her head indignantly. "What's it *like?*" she demanded.

Parker seemed irritated. "Never having been there, I couldn't tell you for certain. What do *you* think it's like?"

Lizzie said she thought it would be like a picnic, with people sitting around under the trees, and with very white tablecloths spread out over rich green grass. She said that was how she had always thought of it.

Parker asked Stone how he thought of heaven and Stone said he never thought of it.

Parker gave him a tolerant smile. He then complained about always having pink junket for dessert and Lizzie rapped her knuckles lightly against his head, playfully the way she sometimes did with Stone and Charlie. But Parker became tense. Letting his spoon clatter into his junket dish, he turned and said in a tight, strained voice, "Don't-you-ever-do-that-again," gritting it between his teeth.

Stone looked up from his plate with amazement. He frowned at Parker, then looked at Lizzie, who stood above the stove with head lowered and her lower lip hanging. She had begun to polish one of the broken porcelain gas-jet handles with her apron, looking once over her shoulder and then back down at the stove.

"Hey, what the hell!" Stone said with disgust. "What did she do? All she did was—"

"I know, I know," Parker broke in with a soothing smile. "I know, Jeff. Sorry, Lizzie," he said resonantly. He ate part of his junket and pushed the plate away, smiled again at Stone and then ambled from the room, holding his stomach with both hands and intoning, "Yum, yum, I couldn't eat another drop."

Lizzie's eyes were clouded. She went about the kitchen touching things that didn't need to be touched. When she started clearing away Parker's dishes, Stone grabbed her wrist and held it, looking up at her.

"Why do you think heaven is a place with white tablecloths and green grass, Lizzie?"

"That's the way it always seemed to me," she said. "Lemme go, boy."

Stone dropped her wrist.

"Gawd," she said, "that man don't act like any preacher I ever knew, but my Gawd he sure does know his Bible."

"I'm sure he didn't mean anything by what he said, Lizzie. Don't worry about it."

"Gawd," Lizzie said.

The next day Parker explained to Stone that he didn't like anybody touching his head, white or black, and asked if Stone didn't feel the same way about it.

Stone said he'd never given it much thought one way or another.

If Parker had special interest in Stone, he quickly made it clear that he had special interest in Charlie as well. Rarely did Stone and Charlie eat at the same time, although there were occasions when Charlie, if he was particularly hungry, left William in charge of the taproom for a few minutes before Stone came on to relieve him.

One evening Stone and Parker had just been served their fried fish and succotash when Charlie came in looking exhausted. Even his hair, in which he took such pride, was messed up.

"Chollie, you look terrible," Lizzie said. "What's wrong with you?"

Charlie grinned. "I had a hard afternoon, Lizzie." He went over to the stove where Lizzie was standing and ran his index finger down her spine. "Chollie, I bet I kill you directly," Lizzie said, simpering.

Stone saw the way Parker looked at Charlie and he wasn't sure what it meant but he knew it was not a look of admiration.

Parker thereupon cleared his throat, bowed his head, waited for silence, then bellowed grace at the top of his mighty lungs.

"Amen," said Lizzie. "Gawd!"

Charlie shoved in next to Stone, across from Parker. "Hey, Reverend," he said, "do you have to scrunch up your face like that when you say grace?"

Parker ignored the question. "What would you say your philosophy of life is?" he asked Charlie.

"What's your-all's?" Charlie retaliated with a grin.

"Show me a bored man and I'll show you a dangerous man," Parker said, munching fish.

"I wouldn't say I was bored exactly," Charlie said. "I find plenty to do."

"I daresay," Parker said. "So I've heard."

Presently Parker screwed up his face again, bowing his head and waiting for silence.

"Christ, he's doing it again," Charlie said. "What are you doing it again for?"

"Dessert grace," Parker explained, picking up his spoon and surveying his junket.

He put down the spoon and raised his eyes and in a mighty voice spoke: "And Jesus went into school and there was a certain schoolmaster who sought to punish the child Jesus and lo! as the schoolmaster's hand was raised to strike, it withered at the end of his wrist!"

"Gawd!" Lizzie said admiringly. "That man sure does know his Bible."

"Apocrypha," Parker explained.

"Gawd!" said Lizzie.

"Holy Christ!" said Charlie.

"Gawd," Lizzie said again.

"Bullshit!" Stone yelled.

"Jeff, you talk that way I smack you," Lizzie said.

Stone looked guiltily at Lizzie. "I'm sorry, Lizzie, but that's what it is."

He saw the look Parker gave him, a fleeting glimpse of contempt, covered quickly with a smile, with a burst of vocal thunder. "So say we all," he intoned in his richest voice.

Through the hole in the wall, William passed a weather book which he said Stone might enjoy. Stretched out on his cot, Stone read that if you stand with your back to the wind, the bad weather is always on the left. He kept reading the same paragraph over and over again, and then Shirley came into his room and sat on the edge of the cot. "Hi," she said. "Are you mad with me?"

Stone closed the book. "Why should I be?"

"Because of Bob?" She looked at him quizzically. "What's wrong? What are you making that face for?"

"I just decided something," Stone said. "I just decided I hate preachers who ask you to call them by their first name. What about—Bob?"

"Are you mad because I'm spending so much time with him?"

Stone shrugged. "If you like him, why should I give a damn? Besides . . . hell—I mean sex and religion are a powerful one-two punch. Hard to beat." Stone grinned at her.

"No sex," Shirley said.

"None?"

"None. I have the feeling he's a virgin."

"Well . . ." Stone felt pleased but tried not to show it. "I'll tell you what else he is. He's crazy. He's a phoney. And I think he also may very well be a son of a bitch."

He then told her of Parker's reaction when Lizzie tapped his head with her knuckles.

Shirley nodded thoughtfully. "You know, though, Jeff . . . He may have been acting. It may have been for effect. I'm sure it was."

"Like hell it was," Stone said. "I was there. I saw it. I'm not an idiot."

"Still—"

"Aw come on Shirley. What kind of effect would *that* have been?"

"Okay, okay, you may be right. But he likes to *try* things. I think he may have been testing you. Or Lizzie. I don't know for sure. He's very strange in some ways. He should have been an actor. I mean he *is* an actor. I had a real interesting thought about him. Can I tell you?"

"Why not?"

"This is what I thought. You know how he does tricks with his voice . . . loud and soft and high and low and then loud and soft even in the same sentence. You know. Doing tricks. Well, I feel he does the same thing with *himself*. With the kind of person he *is*."

"You're getting to know him pretty well, aren't you?" Stone asked. "How does he feel about *you?*"

"He *likes* me. He really does. We've had some very deep talks. About me. He knows I climbed into Charlie's bed."

"That figures."

"He also knows about you."

"What about me?"

"He knows I'm in love with you. He knows I screwed you. I even told him about how you kept my pants in your pocket for me."

"Good God," Stone said. "You really *don't* have much to talk about, do you? What did he say?"

"He said I was far too impressed by it, that it wasn't necessarily all that considerate."

"How would *he* know?"

"You sound jealous, Jeff. You can't imagine how it thrills me to think you're jealous."

"Like hell I am." Stone took her wrist between his thumb and forefinger and looked at it intently. "I'm not jealous, I'm just queer for your wrists." He dropped her hand.

"Are you, Jeff?"

"Yes, I think I am. Listen, if he's the husband you're looking for, go to it. Maybe you and he could go on the stage as a husband-and-wife religious team."

Shirley shook her head. "I enjoy talking to him. That's all. Listen, I'm just a poor dumb little bitch from the coal mines. Let me have some talks with interesting people, will you?"

"Who's stopping you?"

When she had gone, he picked up the weather book, reading once more that if he stood with his back to the wind the bad weather would always be on his left.

Presently he realized that he had dropped the book to the floor, and he was staring at the hole in the wall, muttering, "Come on you bastard, write. *Write.* Do what you're supposed to do. Be decent."

It was the first time in his life he had ever called his father a bastard, even in his mind.

In the dark he watched himself on the small, covered front porch of the rowhouse. He was probably five years old and it was raining. It was nearly six o'clock on a summer's evening, and he was standing on the porch as he did every evening, watching for his father to come home from work, watching for the car. His mother was in the kitchen and there were no brothers yet. His mother came out to the porch and asked the rain, rain to go away so that Jeffrey could go out and play. She went back inside and he stood there, watching for the car through the silvery rain. The wet cobblestones of the street gleamed. At the top of his lungs he shouted happily, confidently, "DAAAAADDDD—come on—ho-ommmmm." His mother came from the kitchen and stood just inside the screen door, telling him he shouldn't shout so loud. She stood inside the screen door, smiling at him.

Stone lay on his cot in the dark, staring into the past at the wet empty cobblestones.

* seventeen

It seemed hard to believe that Charlie could be influenced by the likes of the Reverend Parker, yet a change had occurred in Charlie and when Stone thought about it he realized that it could be traced back to the evening when they all had supper together, when Parker had asked Charlie his philosophy of life.

From a cheerful, no-good bastard, from a jolly, dimpled satyr, Charlie turned moody, and whether by coincidence or not the cash once again began to come up short.

For three nights in a row there were heavy shortages, and on the fourth night, when the shortage totalled eight dollars and thirty-five cents, Mr. Perry glared at Stone and then counted the money again, making stacks of the quarters and dimes and nickels on the bar. When it still came out eight dollars and thirty-five cents short, he angrily swept the money into the sack, choked the sack with the drawstring and looked darkly at Stone. With an imperious frown, he stated that he was not in business for his health and said that money, since it had no wings, could not simply fly out of the cash register.

"Am I right?" he demanded.

Stone said yes, it would certainly seem so.

With his tan pongee suit, Mr. Perry often wore an orange necktie. He wore one now, along with an expression of fearful anxiety and alarm that money rightfully his should be denied him.

"Then where in the God's name is the money *going?*" he demanded.

Stone said he didn't know, although he thought he did know.

"Well, it's got to stop," Mr. Perry said and stalked out.

Stone locked up the taproom and went to his room. In a few minutes he heard heavy thudding footsteps along the corridor. Mr. Perry was looking in at him through the screen door. "Do you ever leave this hotel when you're off-duty?" he asked.

Stone said not often.

"What do you know about this fellow Charlie?"

Stone said not very much except that he knew Charlie enjoyed his job and was popular with a great many of the customers.

"I've heard he falls asleep on the job," Mr. Perry said.

Stone said nothing.

"What in the God's name do you have your shoes filled with sand for?"

Stone told him.

"That's the most ridiculous thing I ever heard of," Mr. Perry said. "There are no rats in this hotel. Kitty Tom chased them all away. There used to be a few before we got Kitty Tom, but not any more."

Stone nodded. Then he said, "Mr. Perry . . ."

"What is it?"

Stone didn't know what it was. But it had to do with wanting to tell Mr. Perry not to worry so much about money, and that he should never have fired Mr. Gaston and that he should let everybody eat upstairs together. "I'm sorry about the money being short," he said.

"Well, you dairned well should be," Mr. Perry said and stomped off into the night.

The next evening Charlie came on to relieve Stone promptly at six, looking resplendent as always in his clean white barman's jacket, his blue-black hair freshly greased and carefully combed, his face shaved to the bone. He seemed reluctant to let Stone leave. He kept him there with questions he did not ordinarily ask, such as how business had been and whether any of his girls had been in asking for him.

"You know something I've decided, Jeff? I'm no damn good." Charlie grinned very ruefully. "You know what I think I'm gonna do when this places closes? I think I'm going to learn how to fly an airplane and go over to England and help out those poor bastards in the RAF. They could use some help, they sure as hell could."

Charlie then talked pensively of college, the year 1936, and of how good a man could feel at the start of the lacrosse season. He could remember the fine bracing sting of the March wind on his bare legs when he took off his sweat pants and ran in his lacrosse shorts, while the coeds and crocuses looked on. At fraternity meeting there was an argument over whether members of the lacrosse team should be allowed extra milk at meals. Some fraternity members who were non-lacrosse players objected but were overruled on grounds that varsity lacrosse players brought luster to the fraternity name. Charlie smiled reminiscently, conceding that it was a silly thing to argue about, but that it was all tied up with his memories of lacrosse in spring.

Stone said he was hungry and was going to eat. As he left,

Charlie was standing behind the bar, a bottle of beer in his hand. He was smiling and his cheeks were dimpled, but it was a sad smile and his eyes had a faraway look.

That evening Charlie took not quite a hundred dollars from the cash drawer and disappeared.

Charlie's replacement was Mr. Perry's own nephew, who arrived so quickly, the very next afternoon in fact, that it seemed clear he had been alerted long since to be ready to jump, although Stone had the feeling that it was himself Mr. Perry had expected to replace, not Charlie.

Mr. Perry's nephew had blonde, crinkly hair and went about all afternoon and evening grinning at people as if he were running for office. His name was Buddy and he was a freshman in college where, according to Mr. Perry, he was very popular and made very good grades. "You'll like him," Mr. Perry told Stone the morning after Charlie's flight. "He's a good clean boy and all."

Buddy made it immediately clear that he was on the look-out for realism and color, and that he had hardly been able to contain himself until he was old enough to be permitted to work in the colorful world of his uncle's hotel. Given his choice of eating upstairs or downstairs, he chose downstairs and he would have, he told Stone, much preferred sleeping in Charlie's old room, but Mr. Perry had promised his mother that he would not have to sleep in the basement because he was not used to such things.

On the evening of his arrival, Buddy stayed in the taproom with Stone, learning the ropes, as he described it, and during the evening he talked incessantly. He confided to Stone that he had been going with the same girl ever since the age of thirteen, which was when he had met her in tap-dancing class, but now he was getting a little tired of her and had a desire to branch out and possibly even taste "a little strange fruit," admitting, however, that to this point in his life he had tasted no fruit whatever, strange or otherwise.

Buddy also volunteered the information that he was a political science major, although what he told Stone was that he was a "polly sigh" major. As they locked up that night, he said that so far as real education was concerned, he was sure he would get more of it working in the taproom and hanging around in the basement than he ever would get at college.

The cash checked out to the penny.

What with the callous dismissal of Mr. Gaston and the abrupt departure of Charlie and the equally abrupt arrival of Buddy, Shirley told Stone that Mr. Perry had now experienced enough personnel changes to be satisfied, at least for the time being.

But the day after Buddy's arrival, one of the chambermaids quit, prompting Mr. Perry to tell everybody that she was no good and that he had planned to fire her anyway.

However, she quit on a Saturday night, which was the very worst time for a chambermaid to quit, since the weekends were always very busy with check-outs and check-ins. "She left me in the lurch," Mr. Perry said—repeating, however, that he had planned to fire her as soon as he was able to get around to it.

As a result, Lizzie was pressed into service on Sunday morning, announcing that she was as glad to get back to her old floor as a "possum going to his nest."

Shirley said that Mr. Perry repeated this remark to a number of guests, who laughed.

For lunch that day, the downstairs help ate food normally reserved to the upstairs help. It was carried downstairs by William. At lunch, therefore, Lizzie, instead of being downstairs cook, was herself one of the downstairs help who stood behind the lattice partition waiting for the downstairs white help to finish and be gone.

While he ate with Buddy and Parker, Stone could hear Lizzie carrying on out in the passageway. She was describing a couple in one of the rooms on her floor. "Here *she* come . . ." Lizzie said in a squeaky voice, and Stone could see her through the lattice, taking small mincing steps of youth, and then Lizzie said indignantly, "And here *he* come . . ." and Stone saw her walking ponderously, bent over, holding her back. "Wouldn't get out of the bed and *wouldn't* get out of the bed and finally here they come out and he all bent over, must be a hundred, and she nothing but a *baby!* Gawd! Enough to make you sick stomach."

Buddy laughed very hard and kept looking about at the others to see if they got all the nuances there were to laugh at.

Stone had never seen Lizzie so happy and he judged that this must have been the way she was before she got demoted to downstairs cook doubling as bathhouse girl.

Buddy called to Lizzie through the lattice, egging her on, whereupon Lizzie inhaled and exhaled one great laughing sigh.

"My uncle's been telling us about Lizzie for years," Buddy explained to Stone and Parker. "In our family she's sort of a legend, you might say. Boy, what a character."

Parker lit his pipe, rocked back in his chair and looked thoughtfully at Buddy.

When Stone came back that evening for supper, he found all the white help gone and the colored help seated at the long table, listening to Lizzie. William told Stone it didn't matter about his being late because supper was sandwiches from the drug store and that his sandwich was on the counter

and just to go ahead and take it. Stone unwrapped his sandwich and, standing next to the stove, began to eat it. He
asked Lizzie how things had gone and she waved her hand
wearily and said, "Tell 'em to send the wagon, just tell 'em
to send the wagon." She shook her head. "It don't even have
to stop, I'll just hop on as it goes by."

The others laughed and Stone judged that what she meant
was that she was weary to the point of insanity, although
happy withal.

Buddy had already eaten. Apparently fearing that he might
miss something, however, he now returned in time to hear
Lizzie's remark about the wagon. With a knowing grin, he
said, "What wagon, Lizzie? Hey, Lizzie, tell us what wagon
you're talking about. William—what wagon is it she's talking about? Oh! *I* see!" Buddy laughed appreciatively and
looked at Stone to see if he too was laughing.

Having obviously heard of Lizzie's erstwhile skill at clean-
ing bathtubs and toilets, Buddy now asked her whether she
had maintained her old speed. She gave the same great sigh-
ing, dutiful laugh, two notes in duration.

"Tell us about the assick, Lizzie," Buddy said. "Did you
use a little assick?"

"*Ah*-haa," Lizzie breathed.

William said, "Who's he getting, Miss Lizzie?"

"Who who gettin'?" Lizzie asked with a scowl.

"Who who *who* getting?" Buddy asked with a grin.

"Ah-haaa," Lizzie sighed, managing to smile at Buddy.

"Who Mr. Perry getting?" William asked.

Angrily Lizzie said that if Mr. Perry got anybody to take
her place as chambermaid with the season so near an end, she
would knock his head off, along with the head of her replacement.

Buddy was convulsed with laughter.

Lizzie was boastful and happily tyrannical, and Stone thought once again that this must have been the way she was in the days before her demotion.

However, an hour or so after she finished eating supper, Lizzie died in her room of a heart attack.

Stone learned of her death the following morning. He also learned that since she had died on a Sunday night, when things were still quite busy, and since also there was no funeral parlor in the resort, her body had been taken for the night down to the ice house, where it lay with two marlin that had been caught that day.

Her funeral was scheduled for Tuesday afternoon. On Tuesday morning, Stone awoke to the sound of a rustling at the wall, and then the sound of a letter hitting the floor.

He jumped up from bed and picked up the letter, calling out his thanks to William and then sitting on the edge of his cot, seeing that it was from his father.

For a few minutes he just sat there, holding the letter in his hand. Then he opened it, reading:

> "My dear Jeff,
>
> Sorry to take so long in writing but what with one thing and another things have been really hectic around here and I've been on the go every darned minute. Last week I had to be in Richmond almost the entire week, and the week before that we had a crisis in the office, one of the girls got sick and another one had to stay home and take care of her husband, so it's been just one thing right after another. I hope things are going well with you, and that you're getting out on the beach and not working too hard. I'm hoping things will ease up around here enough so that I can get down to see you again before very long but as far as your offer is concerned I don't see how I can very well get away for any extended trip any time in the immediate

future. I don't want you to think I'm not grateful for your offer. I think it's very good of you to suggest it, but I just don't see how I can very well take advantage of it right now.

You'll remember that I promised to send you that article about going into the army, and I finally located it. I'd put it in my brief case to save for you and forgot I had put it there, but anyway here it is, and I hope you get something out of it. I think a lot of it makes good sense.

From what I read in the paper, you must have had quite a crowd down there last weekend and I can't blame them because the heat here has been terrific and the forecast is no help either, not even a thunderstorm to help out. But there's usually a little breeze on the side porch at night and we have a couple of electric fans going, so all in all it could be worse, although it's plenty bad enough. There was a picture in the paper this morning of people sleeping on the ground down at Hain's Point.

Let us hear from you when you have a chance and I'll hope to see you before very long. All love, devotedly,

Dad"

* eighteen

Stone went to Lizzie's funeral. Except for the evening he drove Lizzie to her house in the field, it was the first time he had been away from the beach the entire summer.

The funeral was held in a small shabby church just down the road from her house in the field, not very far from the

Coca Cola sign that covered one whole side of a store.

Stone rode over with William and together they approached the casket, which stood open at the head of the center aisle.

Flowers were decked high on both sides of the casket and among them, William whispered, were quite a few sprays from white people.

Stone stared into the casket, not liking the way Lizzie looked, not liking the fancy brown lace dress she wore. The undertaker had done poorly because he had tried to do far too much. Her face was heavily rouged. Her lips were thinned to an unnatural line and stained deep purple. So wispy and grey in life, her hair now was dark and oily, arranged in ringlets and smoothed tight to her head.

William placed Stone in a pew by himself, then left to join members of his own race.

Near the front, in a separate pew, were Mr. Perry and Buddy, his nephew. Stone sat three pews behind them.

Buddy kept looking all about the church, very curiously, eyes full of light. Mr. Perry lowered his nose into a huge white handkerchief and blasted one raucous note. Buddy smiled faintly.

When Mr. Perry turned his head, Stone was surprised to see tears in his eyes.

Stone sat hating the undertaker for using the rouge. He could see dust floating past the open windows, and through the dust he could see her house, empty and top-heavy in the sea of weeds.

The choir began to sing with a sad, electrifying beauty. When it stopped the song of a mockingbird remained, a liquid, manic coda sailing through the open window.

Stone sat motionless in his pew, gazing at the back of Mr. Perry's neck. As the service progressed he felt swift harsh stabs of something that began as pity and sorrow but which became rage.

He felt the rage pulsing through his body, starting in his shoulders and coursing swiftly down his arms to his hands, which lay curled in his lap.

His rage was directed at the undertaker for using the rouge, for trying to hide the truth, for trying to grind in, smear on, a spot of color that would give her life garnish, asking all to overlook what her life had been, asking all to believe that her years had been spent some other way, not in moving her body ponderously through the motions of toil, kneeling before a toilet to scrub clean all traces of the white man's defecation, genuflecting at a tub on aching knees to scrub the tub clean so that it would be an inviting, pristine vessel for a white body's repose.

This had been her life. In an easier job she had found lower personal esteem, had sat yearning for the glory days of scrubbing stains from toilet and tub and then, when the opportunity came, she had responded with eager gratitude to rise, like an aged, ponderous bird with a bursting heart, fluttering and straining, flying one last time before dashing itself to death against hard, cold porcelain.

And then had lain in the ice house until the undertaker could make amends to her, until he could make it clear that she was distinct from the marlin, by waving and oiling her hair and rouging her cheeks and painting her lips purple and dressing her in brown lace.

With three quick chords on the upright piano, the choir began to sing again, and when it was finished the minister called her Miss Lizzie and said she had lived a good life. "We had her amongst us," he said to the stained ceiling, "and now be she gone."

Stone looked at his hands, spreading his fingers wide, and

it seemed as he watched that his fingers had a life of their own.

His fingers clawed their way inside his jacket, touched his father's letter and returned to his lap.

Hearing the minister, he watched his mother kneeling at the border of a flower bed, covering her hands with dirt, saying the best medicine for misery was to dig in the soil, the earth. He saw her fingers coated with a moist film of earth and then soon the earth dried to become a skim of pale mud that somehow did not look out of keeping with his mother's pale, lightly-polished nails. She sat on the glider on the side porch and looked at her nails. Behind her head, vines climbed the screen and through the vines he could see the junior high school, far away, high on a hill. In fall, winter and spring he had run all the way to school and all the way home, dribbling his basketball on the sidewalk as he ran. The basketball was a present from his father. His mother looked at her fingers and said it had been hot in the sun.

Near the front of the church, a deep male voice sobbed.

Heat moved in through the open windows, spreading through the church. Pasteboard fans, advertising a beauty parlor, flurried and grew still.

The minister's voice rose, striving for the tone of thunder but it was thin, without power, without thunder. He said that Lizzie had done the Lord's work. At the behest of the Lord, she had let acid flow over stained porcelain and scrubbed and scrubbed. The Lord, said the minister, cared not how menial the earthly task. We must accept what the Lord visits upon us. Nobility lies not in the nature of the task but in the response. Clean porcelain is its own reward.

Stone sat looking at his clawing hands.

Several times the minister was interrupted by one or another of the mourners, who cried out, "Goodbye, Miss Lizzie, goodbye, dear heart."

Stone felt forces converging, unfamiliar forces pressing in from a shadow world, giving him permission to strike blindly because he knew not where to strike, asking him to move without direction but above all to move, because to remain motionless, fettered by pale virtues, was torture.

He would shove his father from the dung-heap and himself climb to the top, to shake his lance at the sun and bellow with rage.

The minister said, "Our father . . ."

Stone moved his lips. "Our father . . ."

"Who art in heaven . . ."

"Who art nothing and nowhere . . ."

Saying the words, he felt a shiver of fear because of the rage they contained, and the defiance and the hatred and renunciation. Saying them, he felt naked, alone in a world where he had never dwelt, and where he would now ask himself to dwell without God or father.

The hand of restraint, of guidance, had been removed, and his shoulder felt cold.

"Thy will be done . . ."

"For thine is the power if not the glory . . ."

Stone turned his clawed palms upward. He would speed to freedom by a flight into hell. He craved speed above all, speed and oblivion, an arrow-man moving for the sake of swift movement, to move fast and with disregard, to expect and even hope for the splintering crash, to cause a crash for the sound it would make, for the relief it would bring, and the punishment it would bring, the hope that it might bring atonement, for then a pattern of order might be restored.

In this, perhaps the last summer of his life . . .

But even as he heard the crash he would make, he knew it would be nothing without God and father to hear its sound and be daunted and demeaned by it, humbled by it, so that he knew he was not free and wondered if he could ever be.

The lid of the coffin was closed. The mourners sobbed goodbye to God's own chambermaid. Mr. Perry blasted once more into his handkerchief and turned his head, weeping as he watched the slow flight of the casket down the aisle.

Thinking of what Lizzie had said about clean white tablecloths spread over rich green grass, Stone moved down the aisle and out into the August light.

∗ nineteen

Alone that evening in his room, Stone lay looking at the curved shadow his lamp threw on the ceiling. In the lighted part of the ceiling there were cracks and smudges. At the edge of the shadow there was a string of cobweb which moved slightly and stopped moving, then moved again, stirred by a faint breeze which Stone, on his cot, could not feel. He knew it was a hot night because there was sweat on his face and earlier he had heard people talking about a land breeze, which always made it hot. The cobweb was black with filth, which he supposed gave it more weight, although he could not be sure whether this would make it more or less likely to move in a zephyr.

Presently he went out and wandered alone on the boardwalk. Although it was near midnight, the concession and amusement areas were crowded. He felt detached, invisible, moving unseen and without sound, while the faces moved steadily past him, faces bathed in lavender light, all with the look of quest, filled with despair in a place of pleasure.

He saw the girl standing before a plate glass window, a frail girl looking malnourished, her long dark hair falling over one eye in a pitiable imitation of Veronica Lake, dark lipstick gleaming, her breasts timorous against the cheap pink sweater. Stone watched as she continued to stare with rapt despair, gazing at cheap trinkets, cheap objects of art, statuettes of Christ fashioned from sea shells and coral, statuettes of the Virgin converted to lamps. Moving closer, he could see now how homely she was. In spite of the long hair, the lipstick, the suntan, she was pitiably ugly. He moved up beside her at the window, feeling a form of drunkenness. "Hello," he said, "my name is Jeff."

Shielded by the massive shadow of the bandstand, they sat in darkness on the edge of the boardwalk, their feet dangling just above the sand.

Her name was Faye and she worked fifty weeks of the year filing letters, and in these, her fifty-first and fifty-second weeks, she had come to the beach with someone she called her girl-friend. This was the final night of the two weeks. At her job she earned $22.50 per week, and she was twenty-five years old.

Taking her hand, he led her down to the water's edge and they walked southward, beyond the concession stands. Sitting beside her, with her head on his shoulder, he told her she was beautiful, and that even though he might never see her again she would know that on this night she had been loved.

"Beautiful? Me?" She snickered with disbelief.

"Yes," he said. "Beautiful. You. You are the prettiest girl I've seen at the beach all summer long."

Haltingly she told him that although this was her last night she might arrange to get down the following weekend, and her voice said that she would move mountains if need be.

Stone said he would be gone back to army camp by then.

Before leaving her on the boardwalk, he told her that whether they met again would be unimportant because she would always know that on this night she had been as beautiful, as deeply loved, as any movie actress, any princess, any houri, any blessed damosel.

"If it wasn't for the draft, what would you do?" Buddy asked in the taproom. "Just go around to a resort and then when the season ended, go on to another one, huh?"

Stone said he wasn't sure.

"What I'd like to do, I'd like to more or less follow the sun," Buddy said, "except I have to get my college degree first. Not that I really care so much. But my parents do, that's the thing."

Stone nodded.

"I don't believe in money really," Buddy said earnestly. "I believe more in people. Now take Lizzie, there was a real character. It's too bad she had to die. Something real passed from the American scene."

Stone wore only his swimming trunks. He held his dark glasses up to the light to see if they were clean.

"My uncle says she died with her boots on," Buddy said, "and that's the way she would have wanted it, and I more or less agree."

Stone put on his dark glasses, letting them slide low on his nose.

"My uncle says she died more or less in her hour of triumph, you might say," Buddy went on, scratching between his shoulder blades. "He said she wouldn't have wanted it any other way. What do you think?"

Stone shrugged. "Who knows? I guess we'd have to ask her."

"I think what he means is that she'd rather have died doing

the work she really loved, than live a half life . . ."

"Being a bathhouse girl and cook," Stone finished. "I can see his point."

"Anyway," Buddy said, "I sure miss her. Even though I didn't know her very long. She added a whole lot. Remember how she used to say assick instead of acid?" Buddy chuckled fondly. "Where are you going? Out on the beach?"

"Right," Stone said.

When he was nearly to her hotel, he jumped from the boardwalk and ploughed through the soft sand down to the shimmering wet sand that was so like a mirror, reflecting heavy chunks of twisted clouds. He began to walk along the water's edge, looking down at the reflection of the clouds. Ahead he saw a towel and white sweater and placed carefully on the sweater were dark glasses. He sat down near the towel, watching as her white cap bobbed in and out of the waves. Presently she let a wave carry her toward shore. She took off her cap, wading slowly through the shallowing surf, tossing her head and shaking out her long dark hair, and then seeing him. "Hi!" She waved. He rose to meet her, noticing the way her body looked in the gleaming black bathing suit, and then looking down at the delicate, high-arched prints her feet were making as she stepped into the clouds that were reflected in the smooth wet sand. "Hi," he said. "I came up to ride some waves."

Gripping her hand tight, he drew her into the ocean until the water was waist-high and then chest-high. Now it was up to her neck, lapping at her chin. Her lashes were wet, her eyes gleamed and her tanned face was as smooth as porcelain. It had a high, polished gloss. The earpieces of her white cap she had flipped up so that the tendrils of hair at the temples were as damp as her luxuriant but carefully tweezed brows.

"Sometimes they come three in a row," Stone said, gripping her hand.

"It's so deep, Jeffrey." Her voice sounded alarmed but her eyes danced. "Let me go back where it's not quite so deep and watch you first."

"Okay." He stood waiting for the wave he wanted, glancing over his shoulder at her and then back toward the horizon, waiting for the water to swell. When he saw the wave begin to mount, he jockeyed for position before it, and when it began to curl, arching its mighty chest, he swam hard ahead of it, feeling it lift his body and send him skimming toward shore, drifting him to a stop in the shallows.

As he leapt up, she was applauding, smiling. "Okay?" He took her hand again, striding against the pressure of the water, paddling with his free hand. "I'll tell you which one to take and when I say 'go' you start swimming out ahead of it. The main thing is not to be scared of it."

They waited and a wave came that was beautiful but it was too large and looked too powerful for her, so he told her to wait. When the next one began to mount, he told her to get ready and then yelled "go!"

She dived out ahead of it, head down, arms extended stiffly —and then disappeared in a frothing, churning mass of white and green water.

He swam hard after her, reaching her just as she came up gasping. "Did it dump you?" She was choking and spluttering and yet her eyes were unafraid. "Swallowed . . . tons! . . ." she managed to gasp.

Grinning, he picked her up in his arms and carried her to shore. She put one arm and then both arms about his neck. Kicking aside her sweater and sunglasses, he deposited her gently on her towel.

"Jeffrey!" she said breathlessly. "I'm just not sure . . . I'll *ever* be a wave-rider." She pulled the cap from her head and shook out her hair, wild and thick. She laughed, which made her cough again. "I must have swallowed half the Atlantic *Ocean.* It was so *powerful.* It turned me upside down and over and over and I thought I was going to *drown.* It was like being in prison. I must admit I was petrified. Whew! I think from now on I'll just watch. Don't you want to sit here on the towel? You'll get all sandy."

Stone looked deep into her eyes, shaking his head. "No thanks, I'm fine. I'm sorry it dumped you. It was probably my fault." She kept tossing her head, shaking her hair free. "Do you mind if I say something, Mrs. Hopper?"

"I do if you call me Mrs. Hopper. Honestly, you make me feel a hundred years old, Jeffrey." She laughed, and he winced. Wincing, he had closed his eyes, and he wondered if she had noticed, and wondered if she could tell what closing his eyes had meant—that there was something about her voice but particularly something about her laugh, that rasped deep in his being.

"You mean I should call you Ellen?" he asked.

"Please, please call me Ellen."

"Okay, what I was going to say was that you look great in that bathing suit."

She smiled. "Thank you, Jeffrey. Thank you, kind sir."

He kept looking into her eyes with a faint smile and then, briefly, overhead at the thickening sky, the scudding clouds, and then again at her, feeling powerful, waiting for her to drop her eyes in embarrassment but she didn't. She kept smiling back at him until he looked beyond her shoulder, out over the ocean.

"Have you heard from your father, Jeffrey?"

Stone nodded. "I had a very nice letter from him," he said, looking down at the sand between his legs. "He sent me an article telling how to go into the army in the right frame of mind."

She raised her eyebrows. "Really? What did it say?"

"Well . . . it said that inner peace is very important, and also a clear conception of reality, and also strong religious belief. It talked about some survey they took showing that religious soldiers are usually braver than those who are *not* religious . . ."

"Yes . . . I guess that would make sense. Well . . . that was very thoughtful of him. You certainly do have a wonderful father, Jeffrey. He certainly does love you and your brothers, I happen to know that."

"How?" Stone asked somberly.

"Just from things he has said to Larry and I."

"Larry?"

"My husband."

"Oh," Stone said.

"Oh," she repeated with a smile.

"Has your husband been down here with you?"

She shook her head. "We're just recently divorced and he has the kids for the summer."

"So that you could almost say he's your *ex*-husband?"

"Right, Jeffrey."

She then told him that her ex-husband drank too much beer, played too much golf, laughed too boisterously and was generally speaking crude, given to telling dirty jokes that were not particularly funny.

"Why should I be telling you about my ex-husband?" she asked.

Stone shrugged.

She then said that her husband's life had reached a pinnacle in high school, where he was president of his high school fraternity and where she had been president of her sorority. "It was sort of like brother and sister," she said, asking Stone if he understood.

"Not exactly," Stone said.

"Well, what I mean," she said, "is that our sorority was sort of a sister sorority to his fraternity, and his fraternity was sort of a brother fraternity to our sorority."

"Oh," Stone said.

"So it was only natural that he and I should be drawn together."

"Yes," Stone said. "I suppose so, especially since you were both presidents."

She nodded, then looked at him sidelong. "Jeffrey, are you making fun of me?"

Stone frowned. "Of course not. Why should I be?"

"I thought for a minute you were."

Stone shook his head. "Not at all." He got to his feet, grabbed the hem of his trunks and squeezed. "I should be getting back."

"I'm so glad you came. And I'm sorry I wasn't a very good pupil. Next time maybe I'll do better."

"Next time," Stone said, looking into her eyes, "I'm sure you'll perform beautifully."

She extended her hand, and he realized how very fond she was of extending her hand to people, perhaps because it was a slim, patrician hand and she was very proud of it. He took it briefly and dropped it. "So long," he said gruffly and was off.

That night Stone lay on his cot, looking at the ceiling. Next door in William's room there was a party, which consisted of playing the radio, drinking, laughing and talking. Stone watched the cobweb move in the breeze. William told everybody to keep quiet because there was a man next door trying to sleep. "Hey, Stone," he called softly and Stone answered, saying not to mind about the noise.

He heard a girl's voice asking who it was talking through the wall.

"Come right up to this here hole here," William said, "and let me introduce you. Hey, man, this here is Alice."

Alice giggled and said hello. Then William introduced Thurston and Leroy and Katie and John, all from other hotels.

John had a heavy voice, rich and deep, and he also had very precise enunciation. He said, "So this is your communications system then . . ." and chuckled low in his chest.

William said he had planned the party two weeks earlier but then Lizzie died, so he thought he should wait.

John, in his deep rich voice, said, "Death must come to us all," but it didn't sound pontifical.

One of the girls said, "Let's not talk so much about dying," and then the other girl asked Stone if he didn't want to come around and join the party, but William said swiftly, "What he wanna travel all that way for? He already *at* the party."

John asked Stone what he did and Stone said he was one of the bartenders, and John said, "Oh, that's nice." John said he was head waiter at one of the other hotels and that his son was born with one leg shorter than the other, causing him to limp.

John left the party early. Before leaving he slipped his hand through the hole in the wall, chuckling as he and Stone shook hands.

Stone dozed off and when he awoke the party was over and everything was quiet. He turned on the lamp and saw that it was ten past four.

* twenty

From Shirley, Stone learned that Mr. Perry had paid for Lizzie's funeral and also planned to buy her a headstone, although he had not ordered it because he could not decide upon the inscription. Mr. Perry said that no one knew when Lizzie was born exactly, which made it difficult. She had had no family and Mr. Perry claimed that *he* was her family, all she had. At first he had decided to put B-?, D-1941, then decided that it would not sound right. He said that everyone was born in some certain year and that to express ignorance of that year was to deprive the deceased of dignity. So he had now more or less decided to put B-1874, D-1941, because that would make Lizzie's age come out to sixty-seven, which was the age she had seemed to him. He was determined in any event that Lizzie's life should not pass unmarked.

Shirley said that Mr. Perry spent a great deal of time drawing headstones on large pieces of paper. He drew square headstones and low rectangular headstones as well as some that curved at the top. Mr. Perry enjoyed drawing things. He had asked Shirley what she thought of, "Gone, But Not From Our Hearts," and Shirley told him that frankly she did not consider it very original, that the exact same inscription was on the headstone of her poor Uncle Fred, who had been blown up in a mine explosion. She felt she had hurt Mr. Perry's feelings because he thought this inscription was quite good and had in fact just about decided to go with it. Instead he went back to drawing on the sheets of paper again. He was not content merely to mull over an idea. Each time he got an idea he carefully drew a headstone to scale and then carefully printed the inscription. By now he had used up quite a few sheets of paper which he would sometimes leave about the office when he happened to be interrupted by something such as a guest wanting to rent a room, or the vegetable man arriving in the alley. Some of the drawings therefore would blow about the lobby and occasionally the guests would find them and bring them back to the desk, asking Shirley what they were. "Love, Duty and Toil," they would read musingly. "Toil, Duty, Love—I found these over in the Chinese Checkers Room. I guess somebody must have lost them."

Mr. Perry still had not decided upon an inscription but Shirley said he was very happy in his work.

She looked closely at Stone and told him he wasn't listening. He said that he was, asking what Mr. Perry had finally decided upon.

"He hasn't," Shirley said. "That's what I just finished telling you."

Shirley was sitting at the bar in her pink gingham bathing suit. "Listen to this, Stone," she said, reading from the morning paper:

> Search the Kitchen
> Count the Cans
> Check on all the
> Pots and Pans
> To your country's aid oh come
> With your old aluminum.

"That's because they want everybody to turn in their old pots and pans," Shirley said. "It says they need twenty million pounds of aluminum so they can build more bomber planes."

"Great," Stone said. "How's what's-his-name?"

"What do you care, Stone?"

"I care."

"You don't care about anything," she said. "You really do worry me."

"I don't believe it," Stone said. "Every time I've seen you on the beach you seem very happy, sitting there on your blanket with Parker—with Bob, I mean—sort of looking up at the clouds in an exalted way. I'll bet you never thought religion could be so much fun."

"You underestimate him." Shirley shook her head gravely. "He's much smarter than you think he is, Jeff. And much wiser. Maybe if you talk to him he might be able to help you."

"Help me with *what?*"

"With whatever it is that makes you so damned unhappy. I don't even know where you go any more. You're never in your room any more. What in the hell are you doing?"

"I don't know what I'm doing," Stone said. "I'm not doing much of anything."

"Will you talk to Bob?"

"Hell no."

Stone was in bed that evening when Parker came into his room. "Jeff. . . ." Parker sat at the foot of the cot. "You can't keep going on this way."

"What way?" Stone asked.

"I'm here to help you, my son."

"My *son!*"

Parker chuckled. "I've always wanted to say that. Now I've said it—probably not for the last time."

"If it makes you happy, go ahead."

"You're an imbecile," Parker said.

Stone sat up, astonished.

"You're a blight and a dark mark on the face of humanity."

"What in the hell is *wrong* with you?" Stone asked.

"Just testing." Parker chuckled, tapping Stone's leg with

the back of his hand. "Just jabbing a few pins to see if the patient jumps."

"Okay," Stone said wearily. "I realize Shirley put you up to this."

"Yes, but I'm concerned on my own, Jeff. Is it something to do with going into the army? Serving your country is an honor."

Stone sighed.

"Will you join me in prayer?" Parker asked. He gathered his fingertips into a bouquet and applied them delicately to his forehead, closing his eyes so tightly that deep angry wrinkles creased the corners. "Oh Heavenly Father," he prayed, "have pity upon Thy servant Stone. Lead him unto the right path. Let him ponder what the German U-boats have done to our shipping and let him ponder what the Germans have done to the Jews and so forth. Let him—"

Parker broke off with a frown, disturbed by the explosive sound of the toilet being flushed next door in the ladies' room. He looked angrily at Stone as if he considered Stone responsible. "Seriously, Jeff . . . sometimes just talking helps."

"I have nothing to talk about," Stone said.

Parker's eyes narrowed. He stood and paced, describing a circle about the masonry pillar, looking at Stone with concern each time he came around. Circling for the sixth or seventh time, he kept right on going out of the room.

"Crazy son of a bitch," Stone muttered.

"What was that? I *heard* that!" Parker burst in again, but stopped beside the pillar, laughing.

"Listen," Stone said, "not that it matters to me, but are you really sure you're a preacher?"

Parker's face grew somber. He flexed the bicep of his left arm, looked at the muscles that stood like cords along his forearm, and then looked intently at Stone. "You can hardly be blamed for asking, I suppose. Yes, I am. Of course I am."

Parker sat on the cot again. "Listen, Shirley, as you know, cares for you very deeply. And I care deeply for Shirley. So whatever she cares about, I care about, and I'm quite serious in saying that I'd like to help you in any way that I can. Do you mind if I smoke this?"

Parker had taken out his pipe. Stone shook his head. Parker filled his pipe with his sweet-smelling tobacco, tamping it carefully and when he was finally satisfied that it was compact and neat enough he lit it, drawing deeply and squinting at Stone through the smoke. "Quite a girl there," he said.

"Yes," Stone said. "She is."

Parker waited, as if he were expecting Stone to say something more. Stone said nothing. Parker drew at his pipe thoughtfully. "You probably know her far better than I do for that matter," Parker said.

Stone shook his head. "I very much doubt it."

Parker began to nod decisively. "Okay. Look. I realize that it's presumptuous for me even to think I can help you, or even to think you *need* help. It's simply that Shirley asked me to. Okay?"

"I appreciate it," Stone said.

"And I really wish you *would* call me Bob. The fact is, you don't call me *anything*. I've noticed."

Stone said nothing.

"You know, Jeff, sometimes prayer can be of real help. I'm quite serious. Will you join me in prayer?"

Stone shook his head. "I'd rather not."

"Maybe some other time."

"Maybe," Stone said.

"Jeff . . . is there any trouble at home?"

Stone hesitated. Then he said, "No. There's no trouble anywhere that I know of. Except for people all over the world killing the hell out of each other."

Parker got to his feet. Puffing at his pipe, he looked hard

at Stone. "What we must remember," he said, "is that to handle a beast like Hitler—we in turn must become bestial. There's no other way."

In an hour or so, Shirley came down in her pink gingham bathing suit and a white sweater fastened with the top button. She walked close to the cot and her leg was very close to Stone's hand. She was now tan several times over. His fingers moved. "What are you doing with your bathing suit on?" he asked. "It's eleven o'clock at night."

"I know. I'm going to a beach party. Would you like to come with me?"

"No thanks."

"I knew you wouldn't. Listen, did you and Bob—"

Stone sighed.

"Okay, okay," she said. "I don't care what you think, I like him. And Mr. Perry thinks he's the best night clerk the hotel has ever had."

"In history?"

"Bastard! Listen, I put some clean sheets on your bed. Did you notice?"

"Yes. Thanks. Thanks very much." Stone lifted her wrist and kissed it. "Thanks very much, Shirl."

She turned away and went over to his orange crate, picking up his comb. "Do you know there are some teeth missing in your comb, Jeff?"

"Yes," he said. "I can tell there are."

"*Damn* you." She shook her head. "I don't care. You can't make me mad at you any more, so you might as well not try. Do you know the way I can tell?"

"How can you tell, Shirley?"

"The way I can tell is that I don't care any more whether you love me back or not."

She was standing just beneath the cobweb that was black with dirt. He watched it move in the breeze, trailing over her clean blonde hair. "Move a little," he said.

She looked up and brushed at the cobweb. "What I mean is this," she said. "When you love the blue sky, does that mean it has to love you back?"

"*What?*"

"I said, when you love the blue sky, does that mean it has to love you back?"

Stone shook his head.

"All right, laugh," she said.

"I wasn't laughing," Stone said.

"Guess what? My mother and little girl are coming down at the end of the season to take me back. I'm dying to have you see her."

"I'd like to," he said.

"I think you'll like her. Did I tell you that she stutters?"

"I don't think so."

"She does," Shirley said. "A little. But my mother thinks she'll get over it when she gets older."

When Shirley had gone, he lay there thinking of the course he had set himself upon. He had wound himself up and set himself on a course that would lead straight to Ellen Hopper, and although he knew that it might be wrong as once he had judged wrong, and although he knew that it must betray hatred of his father, he was now willing to do the wrong and willing to feel the hate; quite willing now to use himself as a machine, knowing, even though he had been taught the opposite, that from wrong might come right.

But when he turned off his light it was not of Ellen that he thought, but of Shirley's tan skirt and her bare legs and bare feet and her tanned arms in the sleeveless pink gingham blouse, and of her very clean hair and of her little girl who stuttered.

✳ twenty-one

Charlie had left a rich legacy behind and Stone found that Buddy was deeply interested in becoming a legatee.

Buddy had taken to calling Stone "Stoney." Passing him in the corridor, Buddy would shout happily, "What say, Stoneeee, how ya doin'?"

"Hey, Stone," Buddy said. "I suppose you know why Charlie always kept that barstool back in the storeroom, don't you?"

Stone said he did.

"He used to take girls back there and *make* it with them—right on the *bar*-stool," Buddy said excitedly.

Stone nodded.

"That Charlie—boy, he must have been a real stud, huh?" Buddy asked.

When any of Charlie's old girls came in to ask for Charlie, which a few still did, Buddy would say that Charlie wasn't there any more, but would he do?

He would then gaze into the girl's eyes with a look both smoldering and suggestive, whereupon the girls left.

It was Buddy who called Stone's attention to the girl with the strange eyes. One evening at six, when Stone came on to relieve him, Buddy muttered in his ear, "Hey, Stoney, look at what's sitting at that table back in the corner." Buddy made a clicking sound with his tongue.

Stone looked and saw a girl with long dark straight hair and huge dark glasses. A guy was sitting with her but they were not talking. Buddy said it had been like that for an hour. "They just sit there drinking beer," he muttered, "not talking to each other. It's almost like they're not even together. What's wrong with that guy, anyway?"

With a final look over his shoulder, Buddy left to get his supper.

Stone scrubbed the bar, glancing now and then toward the corner. The girl sat motionless as before. The guy with her was wearing a light blue v-neck sweater. When he got up to play the juke box, Stone saw that his dark trousers clung flesh-tight to his lanky legs.

Stone kept glancing toward their table. The guy looked young, he thought, but at the same time somehow looked very old. Lines slanted downward from the corners of his mouth. Blonde hair fell over his brow from a very low side part. His eyes burned with a determined indolence. Once he seemed to be doing exercises with his face, flexing his neck muscles in a peculiar way, at the same time drawing one finger upward along his neck, as if attempting to agitate sluggish flesh and dispel the danger of a double chin. Except occasionally to raise her glass to her lips, the girl did not move.

When the record ended, they left but the next day, when Stone had the afternoon shift, the girl came in alone and took a seat at the bar.

"Beer?" Stone asked.

She nodded. When he had poured the beer for her, she looked into the glass, waiting for the foam to drop. Even with her dark glasses on, Stone noticed something unusual about her eyes. They seemed to bend about the side of her head, reaching nearly to the temples, and it was as if the outer corners had been slashed back, stitched up again and covered over with mascara.

Then she took off her dark glasses and looked at him. "Would you like to sleep with me?" she asked.

Stone felt a tingling sensation, an explosion that began in the pit of his stomach and traveled rapidly downward. Her eyes had stunned him, and even though she immediately replaced her dark glasses he was still overwhelmed. Looking into her eyes had been like looking through windows of clear lavender glass, and somewhere in her depths he had had a glimpse of evil, of license, of sexual machinations performed against flickering light in a subterranean chamber.

With her eyes hidden once more behind the dark panes, he became aware of her mouth, a mouth that he felt would do anything a man asked of it.

His throat was dry. "Tonight?"

She nodded.

He asked where, and she said beach, boardwalk, ferris wheel, anywhere.

Stone felt the explosion all over again.

"What's your name?" he asked.

"Denise."

"Mine is Jeff Stone."

"Okay," she said softly and slipped from the barstool. Stone watched her walk from the room. When she was gone, he took the bar rag and threw it against the ceiling, catching it as it came down. She had not touched her beer, and even to know this started the tingling again.

She had a car and that night they drove up to the dunes, leaving the car and walking over to the beach. As they walked, she told him that the man with her was neither her husband nor her boyfriend, merely a member of her dance troupe.

"Oh," Stone said. "You're a dancer?"

She said she was but didn't seem to want to talk about it, nor about anything.

Under the stars she slipped quickly from her dress. Her body had no soft flesh. Everything was tight and hard. Running his hand over her body was like running a hand over a statue of smooth, warm marble.

She took his hand and held it against her steeply indented waist, dropping it over the hard blazing curve of her hip. But when Stone drew her down to the sand, she tugged at his hand. "In the water," she said, and Stone made love to her in the ocean, borne gently on swelling not yet curling waves.

When he returned to his room that night, he found a note on his pillow saying, "Dear Stone, Where *were* you? love, Shirley." And although he felt he should be stirred in some way by the note it left no impression.

The next day Denise came to the taproom again. All that morning Stone had been chafing with the thought that he had not truly satisfied her, indignantly excusing himself, however, with the reminder that in the ocean, leverage and footholds had been difficult to come by.

When he mentioned this she smiled, and it was the first time he had ever seen her smile. "It was the idea of the salt water," she said, explaining that she had several times made love in fresh water but never before in salt water.

Hard pressed for a suitable reply, Stone nodded suavely and said, "Oh. I see."

"In olden days," she said, "people thought water could cure any malaise. Physical. Mental. Spiritual. Especially spiritual."

"Yeah," Stone said. "I know."

She then told him that she was tired of the beach, having already been there a full week, and asked him if he would like to drive inland.

"Tomorrow?"
She nodded. "Okay, tomorrow."

Stone by now was mesmerized and, as he willingly admitted to himself, might very well, at twenty-two and with limited experience, be in beyond his depth. He knew for a fact that he was now in an area where he could expect no help from James Thurber nor even from Hemingway. The girl represented to him all that was orgiastic, and he felt that rather than consult Hemingway he might better consult St. Paul. Or perhaps Nietzsche.

Consulting no one save Buddy, so as to arrange the time off, he lay on his cot hardly able to wait for the night and next morning to pass. He had trouble getting to sleep. He kept seeing the slit-back lavender eyes that so moved him, and then later, drifting toward sleep, he kept seeing orgies performed in an arena, except that his partner, instead of Denise, was always Ellen Hopper, and she seemed more opponent than partner.

Sitting beside Denise in her car the next day, Stone realized that he had no idea how old she was. Anywhere from twenty-two to thirty-two, he thought, but even if she was only twenty-two she was already far older than any girl he had ever known.

Having said no more than five words since picking him up, she now turned from the main highway and they began to wind deeper and deeper into the back country, through lowland jungles of pine. Even though she wore her dark glasses, he could see how far back the corner of her right eye was slashed. Her hair fell long and straight below her shoulders, and she was wearing a white dress with a very loose skirt. It was very warm away from the beach, and as she drove she pulled the skirt above her knees and fanned with her hand, smiling faintly.

Stone's mouth felt dry. He licked his lips and said nothing, partly, he thought, because he didn't know what to say but mostly because she herself seemed to expect silence, as if the daylight hours were unimportant to her, as if she lived only for darkness.

Houses like chicken coops were straggling along the road and in another quarter mile they entered a town with a broad square the shade of tanbark, baking in the August sun. She parked and they got out and walked. Stone called her attention to the dogs, which he found very strange. They were mongrels but unfamiliar even as mongrels. They were crosses between jackals and greyhounds, lean and yellow, and the square was filled with them.

People shuffled through the square, looking at them curiously. The dogs gathered in front of an A & P. The sun glittered on the greased corners of her eyes and on the hides of the dogs, and on the filthy surface of a drinking fountain from which the dogs lapped water.

She ran her arm through Stone's and walked rapidly, with long, loose, head-tossing strides. They went into a store and had a coke, standing next to a bin of penny candy, inhaling the smell of harness leather. "Come live with me," she said in a low voice.

Stone grinned.

"Does that mean yes or no?" she asked.

"Where?"

"Everywhere," she said. "What does it matter?"

Stone shrugged, tilting his coke in a sophisticated way and saying nothing.

When it was dark they found a roadhouse in the pine barrens and sat drinking at the bar. After one drink, she told him that she was like an amoeba because each time she split, the new fragment lived.

"All the fragments live," she said.

Stone nodded. He felt challenged by the drink he had nearly finished, challenged by the strange things she said, challenged by the need to match her sophistication.

The bar was lit only by candles in hurricane holders and except for the bartender they were alone. Stone stared at one of the candles as if lost in thought, and then said in a faraway voice, as if to himself, "When the lighting is right, a bar is a cathedral."

He glanced at her sidelong to see if she was impressed. Raising her glass, she didn't seem to be.

In a low voice, filled with irony, Stone said, "And whom do I worship?"

She took off her glasses then and drowned him with her eyes. "You can worship *me*. I was serious, don't you realize? I have to be in Havana next week. Come with me."

Stone drained his glass. The chopped ice at the bottom sparkled in the candlelight. "You mean to dance?"

She laughed. "No, I won't expect you to dance."

"I mean, that's why you have to be in Havana?"

"Yes."

She then spoke of Havana and San Juan and Jamaica and Haiti and Lisbon, bursting with impatience, as if the world had not enough destinations, then damned the war for eliminating Cannes, Deauville, Hamburg, Rome.

"I have money," she said. "I make a great deal of money with my dancing. Come with me, Jeff."

Coolly he looked into her eyes, feeling the now very familiar sensation in his groin. He looked down. Her skirt was pulled far above her knees. He put his hand on her leg, and she closed her eyes and let her head fall back.

"I'm waiting to be called into the army," he said.

She laughed harshly, then blasphemed the army, the war,

the world. "If you come with me, the army can't find you," she said.

He nodded impassively. In a sophisticated voice, he ordered two more drinks and when they came he raised his and took a stiff belt. "It's really great to get away from that damned beach," he said.

"Have you been there all summer?"

"God yes."

"What's it been like for you?"

He raised his glass, swallowed and then, as he placed his glass down, he said, "Nietzschean."

She said nothing.

"You know . . ." he said. "Nietzsche."

Smiling, she put her glasses on again and reached for his hand, placing it against the inside of her leg. "Yes," she said, "I know all about Nietzsche."

Stone looked somberly at the row of bottles on the opposite wall, deciding he had better back away from Nietzsche because she might know more than he did. "Thank God the season ends in another couple of weeks," he said, trying a different tack. He shook his head. "It's like an infection."

"What's like an infection?"

"Pleasure infects that place like a fever. The beach. People all start to look the same. They all have the same faces, the same gestures, they say the same things. The sun reduces everybody to the same common fraction, and it gives the same crinkly, sunburn-tightened smile to all the faces . . ." He turned to her and his voice became intense. "Do you understand what I'm trying to say?"

"Yes, I think so."

"So that eventually no face looks different, even though you know there *are* facial differences. Your face is the first one that's really had any impact on me the whole summer."

"My eyes?"

He nodded. "I suppose so. But not your eyes alone."

Taking off her glasses, she leaned forward and kissed him, opening her mouth wide.

Encouraged, he then told her about the night when he had suffered so severely with sunburn, and about his feelings concerning pain and pleasure, and how one had seemed to blur into the other.

This time he knew that he had made a sharp impression. She took off her glasses and looked at him curiously, lips parted, moving her hand slowly along the inside of his leg.

He took her deep into the woods to a tourist cabin.

All through the day her face had been an arrogant mask, and now, in the dim light, he could see an expression, something in her eyes, a smirk that was close to contempt, and yet in its very contempt there was a challenge to sexual battle.

He confronted her, hardly knowing whether he loved her or hated her but it seemed of no importance. Never before in his life had he so felt the desire to inflict sexual pain.

In his hand her neck seemed amazingly slender and vulnerable, but when his fingers tightened, instead of protesting or crying out, she moaned as if with pleasure and let her head fall back, closing her eyes and opening her mouth, letting her body go limp.

What he experienced then was primitive, jarring, rutting, bone-grinding sex that was new to him, because in it there was utterly no love.

It was primeval lust. It was escape to freedom by flight to oblivion, and he was taken down and down into a world where he could not be hurt because there was nothing else but this, no other sensation, no ethic, no dictum, except to reach and probe into darkness, probing and searching out and striking hard and surviving, again and again, crouched in a cave where he was asked to be no more than an animal, yet not-animal because what he felt was tinged with the acute madness that could only be imbued by the human soul. It was Dionysian yet much more, because Dionysus was too much a gamboler, disporting himself cheerfully upon the earth's green surface, and this was a long long descent into darkness, in the company of someone moaning and whimpering with the agony of harsh pleasure, with no other sound and with only the light of twisting flames which threw grotesque, undulating shadows on the bare wall of a cell.

He should have been prepared, hardly surprised, he would think later, by what she asked. But instead he was shocked.

"Hit me," she moaned. "In the face."

He slapped her lightly and she swore at him with complete savagery. "With your fist, God damn it. Hard. Hard." She was gasping. "HARD."

Stone backed away and stood panting against the wall. "No," he said hoarsely. "I can't. I can't."

For a few moments longer she lay there and then moved swiftly, hurling on her clothes and running. He followed her. She was already backing the car around. He grabbed the door handle and got in.

She drove fast and carelessly, although the road was winding and narrow. The beam of the headlights bounced high and low as the car hit ruts.

"I'm sorry," Stone said. "I couldn't do that. I never could."

"Just don't talk," she said.

Crossing the bridge that led back to the resort, she asked softly, "How old are you?"

"Twenty-two," Stone said. "Why?"

She didn't reply. A block from the hotel she pulled up at the curb. "Get out," she said.

"Good night," Stone said and got out. As he slammed the door the car was already moving.

When he got to his room, he found Shirley asleep in his bed. She had left the light on. He turned it off and stood above her, looking down and listening to the delicate sound of her breathing. Even though his room had the darkness of a dungeon, he could see the faint glow of her blonde head.

As he stood there his hand moved, reaching downward, almost touching her hair and then stopping, yet even so he could sense its texture.

Leaving very quietly, he went into Charlie's old room, which was still empty because Mr. Perry had promised Buddy's mother that Buddy would not have to sleep below sea-level amongst the rats and the cobwebs.

The light fixture had no bulb. Stone lit a match and saw that the mattress was bare and the pillow gone. He lay down in his clothes in Charlie's bed, staring into the darkness.

✳ twenty-two

Although he looked for her the next day and in the days that followed, Stone never saw Denise again and was not sure he would even have wanted to.

In spite of its ending, however, he did not regret the experience. He valued it for the insight it had given him into depths he was still tempted to call base, yet which he had begun to suspect might be neither base nor exalted.

Questions tumbled through his mind, questions about himself, about human needs and human responses, questions having to do with good and evil. He knew clearly now that he equated Shirley with good. Finding her asleep in his bed that night, standing above her and seeing the faint glow of her head in the darkness, he had felt that he had come home to something angelic. In spite of all she could do or say, he knew that he could never see her as anything but wholesome, clean, scrubbed and possessed of a sad, little-girl quality that was wistful and totally appealing to what he regarded as the best side of his nature.

It was ironic, he thought, that although to him Shirley represented good, to Parker she undoubtedly conveyed a touch of evil, a fallen woman whom he was reclaiming, doubtless to his own titillation; reclaiming her from the pit of hell which was, to Parker, represented by the fact that she had slept with Stone and had even accommodated Charlie in his good-natured satyriasis.

From his bizarre encounter with Denise there was another value. Even though he knew that in the end she had looked upon him with contempt, the experience had given him confidence. He felt older and more sophisticated, for he was sure that what his father and Ellen Hopper had together could be no more than clumsy, fumbling and sophomoric. To remember what had taken place in the dimness of the tourist cabin was to feel rather swashbuckling and hard-bitten.

It was by now the twenty-second of August. Labor Day that year fell on September 3, and the day after Labor Day the hotel would close, the summer would be over.

If, Stone asked himself, he was so confident of his success with Ellen Hopper, why did he delay? For what ideal combination of circumstances, what astrological benediction?

He let another day pass and then telephoned her, asking if she would have dinner with him the following evening, a

Wednesday. She said she would be busy Wednesday but could make it on Thursday.

More than once in the next forty-eight hours Stone felt waves of self-doubt, when he was convinced that what he planned was not only ridiculously ill-advised but also doomed to failure. He would merely be laughed at, he would be made to look foolish.

And it was impossible not to wonder if the act was not wrong in itself, riding forth with lance outthrust to pierce his father's guts. Once more, however, he was able to convince himself that what he planned was for his father's own good—not merely for the survival of the family but for the good of his father as an individual, because he would be saving his father from spending the rest of his life with such a woman. His father, he was convinced, needed saving, for what his father planned was an act of dereliction, a giddy, boyish, irresponsible escape, and the tipoff was in his choice, his taste. Stupidly, blindly, he had chosen someone inferior to the mother of his sons. For the sake of one so vacuous, he would desert a good wife and break up a family.

In college Stone had read that sexual prowess was enhanced if one ate lettuce and whole wheat bread.

In the downstairs help's dining room the menu was almost always fried fish, and succotash, and junket or sliced peaches. The bread was invariably white.

In a grocery store on one of the back streets, he bought a head of lettuce and a loaf of whole wheat bread. He immediately ate almost the entire head of lettuce and three slices of bread, putting the remainder of the loaf on the shelf inside his orange crate.

On Thursday morning he ate three more slices of bread and took the rest to the taproom.

He had already shaved, so that when Buddy came to relieve

him at six o'clock he would have only to take a quick shower and dress.

Business in the taproom was light, and during the course of the afternoon he rehearsed his approach, sifting and weighing the gambits available to him.

He would, he had already decided, take her first to the Blue Orchid, a sophisticated bar on the boardwalk, and feed her a couple of drinks. The line about a bar being like a cathedral, he felt, was generally speaking quite effective, particularly if he followed it with the question, "And whom do I worship?" He would use a great many polysyllabic words and quite a few aphorisms, the more veiled the better, so as to convince her that he was old for his age and a figure of depth and mystery.

Standing behind the bar, he looked deep into the eyes of an imaginary Ellen and said aloud: "When the lighting is right, a bar is like a cathedral." He shrugged. "And whom do I worship?"

Reaching beneath the counter, he grabbed a slice of whole wheat bread, broke it and slowly chewed it.

Once he got her up to the sand dunes, he would make a great deal of how bright and numerous the stars were, and he would also use the lines about the effect the sun had upon people who stayed too long at the beach.

Munching another slice of bread, he slouched over the bar in a debonair way, moving his face close to where hers would be, and saying aloud and with feeling, "Everything is lissome or glissome, combining gliding with lissome, and day after day the sun keeps spewing down ecstasy rays . . ."

"Who in the hell are you talking to, Stone?"

Startled, he turned. Shirley had padded in from the store-room and now was facing him with an expression of astonishment.

"Nobody," he said. "Why don't you start wearing shoes?"

Grinning, she sat on a barstool, wearing the same middy blouse dress she had worn on the night she cried. "What's the matter, Stone, have you cracked up?"

Stone shook his head. He reached for another slice of bread and then put it back, feeling that he had probably reached the point where another slice, instead of helping him toward his goal, might do nothing but make a hard tight wad in his stomach.

"You know something, Stone? Sleeping on that bed of yours is like sleeping on a slab. With a potholder for a pillow. Why don't you get yourself a decent pillow?"

"You want a coke?" Stone asked.

Shirley shook her head. "Guess what else? Parker just asked me to marry him."

Stone frowned. "What did you tell him?"

"I told him I'd think about it."

"Well . . . how do you feel about it?"

"A lot of ways," Shirley said.

"Have you slept with him yet?"

"Yep."

"How was it?"

"Lousy."

"Well that's too bad," Stone said, pleased.

"But I *do* like him. He's done a lot for me. Like increasing my understanding of the Bible, for instance. Hey, Stone, do you know something—you're well-stricken with years. At least you *act* like it."

Her wrists were crossed on the bar. He gazed at them.

"There's one thing about the Bible that gripes hell out of me though," Shirley said. "Do you know what Bob says? He says that when my husband used to hit me I should have turned the other cheek. That would have meant I had bruises on *both* cheeks, that's all that would have meant."

Shirley placed her hand tenderly against her smooth tanned cheek.

"It would be wonderful if I could raise her in a nice neighborhood and live in a nice house and subscribe to magazines and all that kind of stuff," Shirley said.

"Well . . . I'm sure Parker could do all that for you," Stone said.

"Yeah, he's going to be rich some day, I'm sure of it. He'll probably have his face on magazine covers and a national radio hookup and everything."

"Great," Stone said.

"He told me about a cross he'd like to have that's a hundred and fifty feet high and all lit up with purple light bulbs."

"Well . . ." Stone shrugged. "When you pass the collection plate in front of a cross like that you can hardly miss."

"Don't be sarcastic," Shirley said.

"I never thought about you as the wife of a preacher," Stone said.

"What did you think of me as?"

Stone noticed how very clean her tanned hands were, how clean around the nails, and he wondered if it was from being in the salt water so much all summer long. "Nothing," he said.

"Thanks, you bastard. Listen, if I do marry him, will you give me away? Like a father is supposed to do?"

"Come on, Shirley."

"I'm serious," she said.

"I'm too young to do anything like that," Stone said. "Besides, you've already got a father."

"I wouldn't let that bastard even come near the wedding. He gave me away years ago, about twenty-one years ago to be exact. The hell with him."

Stone went back to the storeroom. When he returned she was looking at a newspaper. "Hey, Stone, did you see this?

Listen. 'Private Kenneth Wilkinson, who is recognized as the army's champion movie-goer, arrived in Hollywood yesterday from Fort Lewis, Washington, for a six-day whirl in the film capital. Wilkinson was welcomed by six starlets. He saw 245 feature-length movies during his first eight months of enlistment.' "

Shirley grinned, pushing aside the newspaper. "See? You could do that. When you go into the army, *you* can do that, Stone."

"Shirley, listen. . . . Are you *seriously* considering marrying Parker?"

"Of course not," she said. "Jeff . . ." Her eyes became clouded. "Do me a favor. Take me some place tonight so we can talk."

"I can't tonight, Shirley."

She looked stricken. "It means a great deal to me, Jeff. Please."

His face twisted with concern. "I can't, Shirley, no kidding. I would if I could, but I can't."

"Why not?"

"Because . . . I have to do something."

"What is it?"

Stone took a deep breath. "Something."

Shirley shook her head sadly. Slipping from the barstool, she padded toward the door. She paused and looked back at him. "Well, if you love the blue sky and you know the blue sky doesn't want you to look at it—hell, that's not it exactly. Okay the hell with it."

* twenty-three

At supper time the ocean always looked huge and desolate because everybody had gone in for the evening.

She was waiting for him on a bench in front of her hotel, staring out at the empty ocean. When she saw him, she smiled. "Hello, Jeffrey," she said. "Don't you look *nice?*"

Stone walked beside her thinking, bitch, whore, bitch, whore, hating the dryness of his mouth and hating her for the forbidding, unassailable, polished, older-woman beauty of her face against the grey ocean.

"Have you ever been to the Blue Orchid?" Stone asked. "I thought we might have a drink first."

They sat at the bar and Stone explained that the Blue Orchid was the nearest thing to sophistication the resort could offer. As evidence of its sophistication, he mentioned the dim lighting, the long black mirror behind the bar, the huge paintting of the blue orchid overhanging the black mirror, the candles that guttered next to the bowl of pretzels.

There were also the whores who hung out at the Blue Orchid, tanned, lissome whores in flowered dresses, who moved to and fro.

The facade was open to the boardwalk, open to the southeast wind, and the candle flames danced in the breeze.

She asked for a Manhattan and seemed surprised when he ordered Scotch for himself. "Your father told me you never drank anything but beer, Jeffrey." She smiled.

Stone shrugged. "Ordinarily that's true," he said. "But at school last year I started to drink Scotch now and then. I like it."

When their drinks came, he sipped the Scotch, feeling it burn his insides, feeling it begin to saturate all the slices of whole wheat bread.

She began to talk rapidly, non-stop, and Stone wasn't even aware of what she was saying. He was aware, however, of the mocking look that came now and then into her eyes, and aware that her hand came down now and then on his wrist.

She wore floppy open cuffs of white linen that cut a diagonal line across each tanned wrist. Again her hair was parted in the middle, and again he thought of her face as two identical halves of a face. As earrings she wore a couple of very large silver hoops. They glittered in the candlelight and they looked very shiny and new. He wondered if they might have been presents from his father. He saw his father in the earring store, his face boyish and eager, intent upon picking out earrings she would like.

And then he was hearing her.

"If you ever meet him," she said, "and I hope you will some day, I want you to watch his coordination."

Stone nodded. She was speaking of Tommy, her nine-year-old son.

"You can see it just in the way he moves," she said. "He's so beautifully coordinated for his age, I know he's going to be a tremendous athlete. I really don't know where he gets it from. Certainly not from his father, because his father is no athlete. He plays golf but that's about all. His father is a slasher. But Tommy just sort of flows, do you know what I mean, Jeffrey?"

"That's wonderful," Stone said.

"You remind me of Tommy," she said. "You walk beautifully. Did you know that?"

"It's something I never thought about." Stone turned to her. "You're very aware of—the way people walk, aren't you?"

"Yes," she said. "I've always been interested in the way people walk . . . and move . . ."

She sipped her drink. Each time she raised her glass, one floppy white cuff slid all the way to her elbow.

"Now Mary," she said, "she's a different story. She has *no* natural athletic ability whatever, but she's such a wonderful, cheerful kid that it doesn't matter."

"How do you think that will affect her sex life? When she grows up?"

Her hand was on his wrist, and she was looking at him quizzically, her lips parted. "What on earth do you mean, Jeffrey?"

"I mean if she's all that cheerful, do you think she will attract men sexually?"

She took her hand away. "Well that's one I'll have to think about for a minute."

"Okay." Stone drained his glass. "While you're thinking about it, I'm going to order another drink if you don't mind."

"Not if you think you can handle it," she said. "I don't want your father accusing me of getting you intoxicated."

"Hell," Stone said with contempt.

"I'm trusting you, Jeffrey." Thoughtfully she sipped her drink. "Is what you're saying . . . that if a girl is *cheerful* . . ."

"I'm not really saying anything," Stone said. "I'm just wondering."

"I don't see why a girl should be less attractive just because she's cheerful."

"Well, you may be right."

"You're such a *funny* boy, Jeffrey. I don't quite understand you." Again her hand went to his wrist. "But I like you."

"Thanks, Ellen." By now he had his second drink and he could feel the Scotch getting to him. Watching the wild dance of the candle flames, he felt that it was time to throw it at her now.

He separated a pretzel into its component loops, breaking them off cleanly. Watching the flames, he said in a low voice, "When the lighting is right, a bar can be a cathedral." He looked into her eyes. "And whom do I worship?"

Her eyes danced. "Are you looking for somebody to worship, Jeffrey?"

Still looking into her eyes, he nodded gravely.

"Why, Jeffrey?"

"Everybody needs somebody to worship, Ellen. Don't they?"

He watched the candle flames flutter and bend double, fighting to reach the tallow.

"Don't they?" he repeated softly. He held a loop of pretzel close to her mouth, still looking into her eyes. "Look. I made this just for you. Would you like it?"

Smiling, she opened her mouth. Deliberately, sensually, he inserted the circlet of pretzel between her lips, placing it upon the tip of her tongue. "Thank you," she said.

"Thank *you*," he said. "Thank you very much."

"For what?" she asked, chewing delicately.

"For saying, 'thank you' and then letting it stop right there," he said. "For not saying anything more."

She took a cautious sip of her drink and her white cuff slid. "This is a nice place," she said. "I like it. I'm glad we came here. I'm having such a good time, Jeffrey."

"I'm glad, Ellen. Do you know what I mean? About speech? Take my father for example. My father knows the language of words well enough, but the language of silence not at all."

She frowned. "Your father loves you and your brothers," she said. "You have no idea. I know he's been a wonderful father to you."

"Why do you say I have no idea?" Stone asked, breaking up pretzels. "I *do* have an idea. There was one Christmas when I was about fourteen when he went out at four in the morning to an all-night drug store to buy a present at the last minute— to make the presents come out even for me and my brothers, because my younger brother didn't have quite as many presents as Robbie and I."

Stone stared at the onyx mirror and for a moment he choked up. He popped a pretzel into his mouth and chewed hard.

"He's a wonderful man," she said. "He really is."

"I know," Stone said. "I know. I didn't really intend to bring him up. All I really intended talking about was speech, and silence. It's like making love, for instance."

"I beg your pardon?"

Stone shrugged. "Well . . . when I'm making love I don't talk, and I don't want the girl, the woman, to talk either. And yet if it's good, then the words that could flow! God! It's like music. You can't talk *music*. Can you?"

"No, I suppose not," she said, looking over her shoulder. Suddenly her voice became ugly and whining. "But I still don't like to hear you criticize your father. Because I know how much you boys mean to him."

"Gosh," Stone said. "I didn't mean it as a criticism. It's just that—well, you know how it is. When you're young you wonder about your parents, wonder about them being in bed together. Didn't you ever do that? Wonder about *your* parents like that?"

"My parents were quite old when I was born," she said, looking over her shoulder again, this time looking haughtily at one of the whores who had taken a seat next to her at the bar but now restlessly left.

"What I've always thought," Stone said, "is that my father could not really be a very good lover because he *talks* so damn much. I'm sure he must sweat a lot and do a lot of heaving and hauling."

He watched her face. He saw her lips tighten and then part, and tighten again. Her lips seemed to be wavering with indecision.

"Look," he said, "I don't mean any disrespect for my father. I'm very fond of him. It's just that it's fun to imagine, that's all. I think he'd probably be the type to do a lot of *talking*. He'd say things like, 'Is it okay? Is it okay for *you?* Are you *sure* it's okay? Are you comfortable? I wish there was a little breeze. Do you want me to turn on the electric fan? Oh, gosh—I'm *sorry*. A drop of my sweat just landed smack in your *eye*.' "

Watching her face closely he saw her eyes light up for a brief second, saw her lips curve, and then her face was composed again. "Jeffrey . . ." She slid from the stool. "I have to go to the little girls room."

It seemed, Stone thought, like the end of round one; or the first quarter of a football game. He wasn't really sure how well he had done, although the Scotch was persuading him to believe that he had done well. "Could we have a couple more?" he asked the bartender. These would make his third and her second, and he knew that he had to stop at three, because he knew he had about reached his limit, and the thought of being so drunk that he couldn't carry it off was disheartening. He sighed heavily and looked at himself, at his dark, blurred image in the dark mirror, closing his eyes and silently praying, Dear God, please please let me screw her.

When she returned it was clear that she had had a talk with herself in the ladies room. Nearly bumping into one of the whores as she approached the bar, she said icily, "Oh, pardon me," and then, at the sight of the fresh drinks, she said, "Oh, Jeffrey, I couldn't—and you shouldn't either."

"This is my last one," he said. "I'm signing off after this one, so you don't have to worry."

She looked at him with concern, and then dubiously at her own drink. "Don't drink it if you don't want to," he said. "Or drink half of it. Do whatever you want to do. Hell."

She touched her glass with thumb and forefinger, not lifting it from the bar, and then touched the tendrils of hair behind her ears. Her lips were tight and her eyes had lost their sparkle, their mockery. Having decided upon the sexy approach that was so natural to her, she seemed concerned now that she had gone too far, and was prepared to act another part, if she knew one.

Primly she raised her glass. "I'll just have a sip or two and then maybe we should eat supper, Jeffrey."

"Fine," Stone said. He looked down at her legs but couldn't see them, because her skirt was pulled down snugly over her knees. "You know, Ellen, the thing is . . . well, do you know what surprises me about you?"

"What, Jeffrey?" She looked very prim. She looked, he thought, about to flee. "What surprises you?"

But he felt sure she would not flee because the thing he had going for him, he thought happily, was that she had to believe that he knew nothing. She had no choice but to go on the premise that everything he said was in perfect innocence of what went on between herself and his father.

And meanwhile, he felt sure, she was still frail enough to respond to flattery, particularly if right behind it he gave reassurance of his ignorance.

"Well," he said, "*frankly*, I never really *expected* to want to go to bed with anybody as old as thirty-seven. Is that what you are, Ellen? Thirty-seven?"

She took a stiffer drink than he felt she had intended.

"Don't get me wrong," he said. "I don't mean any disrespect. I know you're my father's friend, not mine, and I mean no disrespect. It's just that you being as old as you are . . ."

Her eyes seemed smaller. "Do you really think of thirty-seven as old, Jeffrey?"

"Well . . ." He took a pretzel from the bowl and placed it against her lower lip. She took the pretzel from his hand. "Not any more I don't," he said.

She dropped the pretzel back into the bowl.

"It's just that I guess I expected your *body* to be older. I didn't expect your body to be the way it is, Ellen."

She smiled faintly. "What *did* you expect?"

"I don't know. Not this. I mean, you're really something, you really are."

"For my *age?*" She smiled.

"For *any* age. I was noticing when we were riding waves and, my *God* . . ."

"Thank you, Jeff." She took another sip. "Maybe we'd better talk about something else, okay?"

"Of course."

"I just don't know how to take you, Jeffrey."

"In a spirit of friendship, I hope," he said.

"Friendship?" Her eyes lit up. "Really?"

"Absolutely."

"Oh, gosh, Jeffrey." She let her shoulders fall as if with vast relief. "You have no *idea* how wonderful it makes me feel to hear you say that. You just have *no idea*. I suddenly feel very good."

"Well, I'm glad."

"Because that's all I could ever be to you. I mean, no matter how attractive I might find you—and you certainly *are* a most attractive boy—I could never be anything except your friend. You can understand that, can't you?"

"Absolutely," Stone said. "I understand it perfectly."

"I'm so glad. I feel much better."

"Good," Stone said. "Listen . . . how hungry are you?"
She smiled. "I'm never *very* hungry."

"Well, I was just thinking. If you're not too hungry we could order a sandwich and eat it right here at the bar."

"Lovely. Perfect. On one condition. That you don't have any more to drink."

"I don't want anything more."

Stone ordered the sandwiches and while they waited she started to rattle on about the women in England and their trouble with stockings. Because of the shortage of silk, some of them had taken to painting their legs some hosiery shade or other to give the appearance of stockings, she said.

Stone looked past her shoulder. There was not much daylight left. Gazing out upon the ocean, he could no longer make out the horizon.

"That's something I'd personally hate," she said.

"What would you hate, Ellen?"

"Painting my legs. The paint might be harmful to the skin." She grimaced. "How do you feel about the war, Jeffrey?"

"I think it stinks," he said.

"Well, of course. It's horrible. I just hope we don't ever get into it. And maybe we won't."

When their sandwiches came, Stone gulped his, thinking that he should have told the bartender to make it on whole wheat bread, but then thinking that at this point two slices of white bread would hardly make all that much difference. He shook his head vigorously.

"What's wrong?" She was eating her sandwich in tiny, ladylike nibbles.

"I felt a little woozy, I guess. But the sandwich is helping."

"Have you ever had this much to drink before?"

"Oh sure. Plenty of times last winter. Maybe . . . maybe after we eat we should get out of here and walk a little."

"Are you still woozy?"

"It's getting better."

"Here, eat some of mine. I'm not going to eat it all."

He accepted the half she offered. "I'm not afraid to die though," he said.

"What?"

"You were asking how I felt about the war. I'm just saying, I'm not afraid to die."

"Oh, Jeffrey, please don't talk about dying. You're not going to die."

"Everybody is," he said. "The thing is not to be afraid of it. Do you know why? Because it's just simple common sense. I mean, if by the act of not-dying you were saving your life *forever*, then there would be some sense in trying to stay alive." Stone finished chewing and gulped. "But each time we save our lives, all we're *really* doing is delaying the moment when we do die. Not really saving them but just doing a little delaying-action, do you see?"

"I don't really like to think about it."

"Anyway, besides, if we *were* going to live forever, then our lives would become meaningless. Time, for example, would have absolutely no importance. Do you see what I mean?"

She nodded. "You know, you're very smart, Jeffrey. It's unusual—to be so smart and so nice looking."

"*Me?*"

"Yes, you."

"Gosh," Stone said. He wiped his mouth. "Can we get out of here and walk a little now?"

✶ twenty-four

It was almost ten o'clock when they got outside. He walked her northward, past her hotel, and then to the point where the boardwalk ended. Here he jumped down to the sand and held out his arms. "Where are we going, Jeffrey?"

"Wouldn't you like to walk on the beach a little?"

She jumped down to the sand with a grace that he found faintly surprising. "Can I leave my shoes here?" she asked. She slipped off her shoes and put them beneath the boardwalk. He did the same with his own.

They began to walk toward the dunes, and their bare feet made a squeaking sound in the dry sand. "Jeffrey . . . where on earth are you *taking* me?"

Her voice was now girlish, shrill, falling just short of a giggle. It was, he thought, a very horrible voice. She was her voice.

Touching her elbow lightly, he trudged onward until he reached the spot he had chosen for Shirley, and later for Denise, although in the deep darkness he could not be sure it was the same place. "Gosh," he said, "let's rest."

She sat on the slope of a hillock of sand, panting faintly, and he sat beside her, resting his wrists on his drawn-up knees, looking out over the black and white ocean, patting her head lightly and saying, "You're wonderful, Ellen."

"This is so gorgeous. Do you come up here often?"

"This is the first time the whole summer," he said. "There hasn't been anybody I wanted to bring."

She said nothing, and he sat there loving the place he had

chosen, feeling comfortable in the darkness, with the vast dome of stars clamped down so securely. It was a cave of darkness, with its black domed ceiling and its floor of sand and its open mouth looking out upon the dark ocean. It was magnificent, yet he did not feel diminished by its grandeur but instead protected by it.

Simulating a yawn, Stone walked a few paces away, to where the sand was flat, and then stretched full length, resting his head upon his doubled fists. "I'm going to look up at the stars," he said, hating himself for the momentary quaver in his voice. "They're beautiful, they have such tremendous depth. Come on, Ellen . . . you can lie on my arm."

"I'll get sand in my hair," she said.

"Not if you lie on my arm. Come on, I'll keep the damned sand out of your hair."

She said nothing, but didn't move from where she sat.

Stone lay there in silence, listening to the thud of his heart against the sound of the surf. "You know . . ." he said finally, "I enjoyed that, back at the Blue Orchid. Did you?"

"Yes, very much. Are you still woozy?"

"No, I'm fine. You really should see the stars from here, Ellen, no kidding."

"I can see them from *here*, Jeffrey, no kidding." She laughed softly and got up and walked down to the water. He could see her clearly in the white dress, standing motionless, facing the sea, and it was as though she were standing at the mouth of the cave. When she returned she sat on the sand beside him.

"Lie on my arm, Ellen," he said. "Hell, this may be the last summer of my life. You can at least lie on my arm."

"Don't *say* that. It's *not* going to be the last summer of your life."

"It may be."

"Oh, Jeffrey, you're *silly*. We're not even *in* the war yet."

He reached up and began to play with the ends of her hair, letting his knuckles touch the soft skin behind her ear. "Everything," he said, "is lissome or glissome, combining gliding with lissome, and day after day the suns keeps spewing down ecstasy rays."

"What are you talking about, Jeffrey?"

"That's the way it's been at the beach, I guess because I've been here so long. It gets to you. You sort of move from day to day in a gliding motion. You can be conscious of things that are wrong and rotten but it's so nice in the sunlight that there's no pain, no pleasure, no peaks, no troughs."

"Ummmm." She twisted a little, so that now her feet were pointed in the right direction for her to lie next to him. "You look a little like your father, but you're really not like him, are you?"

"I'm not even sure I look like him," Stone said. "When he gets sunburned he's like a tomato." He raised himself on one elbow. "My father has done one terrific thing for me this summer though. He introduced me to you."

"That's very nice of you to say. Come on now, I think we'd better get back."

"This is too gorgeous to leave. Hell, it's early. Come on, lie down, just for a second, and relax."

"I see no point in it, Jeff."

"There's no point in anything for that matter."

"Yes there is. I'm going down to the water and look at the surf."

"Okay, go ahead." He yawned. "I'll be right here."

She laughed, and he felt her hand against his head, tousling his hair.

"If only my father were here," Stone said, "then it would be complete."

She withdrew her hand and for a few moments she was silent. When she spoke it was in a strained voice. "Jeffrey, listen, dear, there's something I want you very much to understand. I mean—I'm proud to have your father as a friend. But you realize, don't you, that that's *all* your father and I are. Friends."

Stone was up on one elbow again. "Well, of *course*," he said emphatically. "Of course I realize that. Hell, my father *told* me that. He told me the same day he took me up to meet you." Stone laughed.

"What's funny?"

"You are. Gosh. What did you *think* I thought?"

"I just don't want you to get any wrong impressions, that's all. It relieves my mind to know you haven't."

"Well it relieves my mind too."

"I should think it would. No boy likes to think of his father with a girl friend . . ."

"Oh, hell," Stone said. "That's only *part* of it."

"What's the other part?"

"Can't you see?"

"I'd like you to tell me."

"Okay, lie down here on my arm and I'll tell you."

"Jeffrey, really . . ." She moved her body a little. "I can't do that. I'll . . . stretch out and rest my head on your chest, okay?"

"Sure. Okay."

She stretched her body at right angles to his, letting her head fall gingerly to his chest. "Are you okay?" he asked.

"Fine," she said, but he could feel the tension, hear the tension and know it was there. Her body seemed rigid. He lay there in silence, aware of his heart again, popping beneath her head, and he looked up deep into the bright galaxies, breathing his prayer, petitioning God for help.

"You said you'd tell me," she said.

"Well, gosh, isn't it obvious? Don't you see why it would relieve my mind."

"Why?"

"Because—if you and my father *were* more than friends, then think of how guilty I'd feel."

"Guilty . . . toward . . ."

"Toward *him*. I'd feel disloyal. Taking somebody he loved . . . up to the sand dunes. I'd be a real bastard."

She remained silent.

"But this way, knowing that you and he are only friends—well, it lets me off the hook. It lets me feel about you the way I *want* to feel about you."

"Maybe you shouldn't be feeling anything at *all* about me, Jeffrey."

"I can't help it. Is it my fault? Listen, shall I tell you something? After I met you, I started coming up to your part of the beach, just hoping I'd catch a glimpse of you and sometimes I'd see you in the water, or walking along the beach, and my God I'd feel lust rising in me . . . like . . . a vanilla milk shake . . . bubbling up in its shaker. My God."

"Jeffrey . . ." She laughed softly. "Let's go now, okay? I don't feel so terribly well myself. I shouldn't have had that second drink."

"I mean," he said, "I couldn't *help* feeling the way I felt about you. And I kept on feeling it, even after I found out how old you are."

"I wish you'd stop saying how old I am . . ." But her voice was lilting, rather than angry.

"I'm trying to tell you, it doesn't *matter* to me how old you are."

"I'm not old," she said.

"I know you're not. Listen, Ellen, I've got an idea. Let's stop talking and just lie here and look up at the sky . . ."

With her head on his chest, he was aware of her perfume

all through her hair. He touched her hair and touched the skin behind her ear again, and then sniffed his hand, smelling the perfume on his fingertips.

"What are you thinking, Jeffrey?"

"Shall I tell you?" He raised himself on one elbow and let his face hover close to hers. Close to her lips, he breathed hard. "I was thinking about the way you're built. God! Are you built!"

She was trying to rise. "Take me back now . . ."

"Take you back, hell," he said in a harsh voice. He was holding her down with his forearm across her throat. He lowered his lips to hers and reached under her dress, moving his hand slowly up her leg.

It was the scream, the shrillness, the sheer ugliness of it that was jarring. Not so much the volume, and not the fact that she had screamed, but the truly horrible sound of her horrible voice.

She was on her feet, smoothing her dress and moving swiftly down to the water. He ran after her. Grabbing her from behind, he lifted her in his arms and carried her toward the surf. "Have you ever been screwed in the Atlantic Ocean, Ellen? Have you? Have you?"

She struggled and then she was free and screamed once more. This time it had the harsh sound of a night bird, and then, on all fours, she was scuttling like a crab, away from the water.

"You don't have to fight any more," Stone said. "I won't even touch you. Forget it."

He sat in the sand with his knees drawn up to his chin, head hanging, breathing hard.

She walked away, headed in the direction of the resort, rapidly at first and then more slowly. He watched the white dress until it faded into the darkness, and then he started after her, jogging in the wet-packed sand.

She had stopped and had turned to wait for him. She was standing with her hands on her hips, and then, as he caught up with her, she turned and started walking again. He walked beside her. "You poor kid," she said softly. "You poor poor little boy."

"Ha! Listen, don't feel sorry for *me*. Feel sorry for *yourself* if you want to, but not for me, by God, not for *me*."

She kept walking. "I've decided something," she said. "I'm not going to tell your father about this. We won't tell anybody at all, is that agreed?"

Stone's laugh was a jeer.

"Just let it be our little secret," she said. "Just something between *us*, and I won't tell a soul. Just so long as you promise me it will *never* happen again. Just so long as you promise me that you will *never* tell your father."

Stone grunted with contempt. "I don't think it would do any good if I did," he said. "Do you?"

He stopped walking then and she kept going, angling away from the water, and he heard the whining sound her bare feet made as they twisted through the dry sand. Presently he could see her no longer.

Stone lay on the beach and looked up at the stars.

At dawn, he walked all the way to the south end of the resort, where an inlet cut through the spit of land from ocean to bay. A seawall of loose rocks ran the length of the inlet, reaching out into the ocean, beyond the line of breakers. He jumped down to the seawall and sat on a rock. Far down the beach, southward beyond the inlet, the green light of a buoy flashed faintly, and as he continued to watch it began to fade as the light of day came on. To the east, out in the ocean, there was a bell buoy, a white eye visible through its iron supports, an eye swaying and careening with the motion of the sea.

The sun rose, skimming the inlet with light-flecks. Just below his feet, the waves swirled and fought their way up among the black rocks of the seawall, retreating in foaming defeat, only to advance, to curl in through the crevices in a long gliding swirl, retreating and again advancing, fighting the rocks. He watched the currents and cross-currents struggling for supremacy. He sat staring intently, trying to separate the water of one current from the water of another.

He thought of his mother, at home, still asleep perhaps; and of his brothers, ready for another day in the public swimming pool; and of his father, up in the attic, in bed alone, perhaps awake by now, eyes open, staring at the wall, staring, without really seeing them, at the pictures of Joe Cronin, Goose Goslin and Heinie Manush.

✳ twenty-five

Stone wished the summer had no ending but he knew it was the last week of August.

He felt driven now to prayer, and on his cot at night he said prayers richly textured with idiocy. From time to time he offered God ultimatums.

Once he saw an image, surprisingly vivid, in which he drew back his fist and hit God hard in the stomach. He heard the surprised whoosh! as the air was forced from God's lungs, and he saw the surprised look on God's face.

In the light of early morning he lay on the beach, his cheek pressed tight against the soft sand, looking out across the ocean. Strange white clouds were marching along the horizon like a parade of small white animals.

Toward midnight he lay in the dark in front of the hotel, far beyond the overlap of light cast by the boardwalk lamp posts. He looked up at the stars, finding the Big Dipper and then, from it, trying to find the North Star, which he could not find, perhaps, he thought, because there were too many bright stars for any one single star to stand out. He wondered about life on the stars and then he saw, moving among them, a light which exactly matched the brilliance of the stars and which looked the same distance away, although he knew that it was not because it moved and now blinked, and on that star, he thought, there was life. It was blinking its way eastward, out over the ocean, and he wondered if it was headed for England, ferrying bombs which would be used to split the skull and strew the entrails of someone who wanted to live on.

With the light off, he lay in his room thinking how it would be to be dead. He wondered how a person would know for sure that he was dead. If he died in, say, Germany, would he stand above himself somehow and see himself dead, lying on the ground; and would he then congratulate himself for having given up his life for his country? For what part of his country? For its trolley cars, its radio aerials, its Burma-Shave signs?

He could see nothing because the room was dark and his eyes were closed, and he tried to hear nothing, although he knew the surf was breaking, and he tried to smell nothing, although he knew the smell of mildew was very strong.

He knew that he was alive because his hand was resting on the clean sheet that Shirley had put on his cot.

He knew that he was alive because William called, "Hey, man," and then up to the hole in the wall came William's friend John, whose son had been born with one leg shorter than the other, and John said that even though his own life was beyond reclamation he would nevertheless like to have Stone's advice on the sort of education he should try to give his son.

Motionless on his cot, Stone thought of the victory Ellen and his father would win, had already won, thought of them in days to come standing together, genital to genital, their bodies all aquiver with fruition and triumph. For a reason he could not determine, he saw himself in kindergarten, and the teacher was saying "Now I take my right foot, shake, shake, shake," and while the teacher picked out simple notes on the piano Stone extended his foot and gave it a shake, and then the teacher said, "Now I take my right hand, shake, shake, shake . . ." And when he thought of his father and Ellen he saw them shaking their hands and their feet, dervishes, shaking and shaking until all the pleasure and victory was shaken from them and they stood motionless and hollow-eyed.

Although he had no further wish to see her, he called her hotel out of curiosity and was told that Mrs. Hopper had checked out.

He wondered if the pain his mother soon would feel might give her strength. Perhaps she would re-marry, or perhaps in the years to come she would live alone, by winter turning up the oil burner by summer plunging her hands deep into the damp earth.

He lay on his cot, letting the defeat, the misery grind into himself, soak his being, letting it stain the innermost folds of his tissue, the hidden recesses of that part of his brain which registered misery and pain, telling himself that he would outface it, that when it had done its worst, worked its ultimate, he would turn with a snarl. If, he thought, he ever did get back from the war he knew now that he did not want a life devoted to economics. Under his father's guidance he had studied to be a business man. Instead he would start over again and study the human spirit, devote his life to the study of pain and pleasure, joy and sadness, good and evil, and try to find the line that blurred them, and if there was no line, then to study the blur.

Only through pain and misery, corruption and depravity, he had read, could the human spirit truly grow. What then was the ultimate growth? And what the ultimate corruption? Perhaps in both instances, death.

For himself there was now, he knew, no further depravity to which he might resort, or none for which he felt fitted. There was murder, but murder was something for which he was not fitted. There was pleading, a plea to his father to be something that he was not, but he knew that he was no more fitted for this than for murder.

Once, very late at night, he looked full in the face of what he had done, tried to do, and found in it no nobility, only arrogance. For a few moments he was standing atop the dung-heap, looking with revulsion at his bare feet.

A letter dropped through the slot in the wall. It was from Mr. Gaston and it thanked him for writing and wished him luck in the army. In spidery, attenuated penmanship, Mr. Gaston apologized for the delay in replying, explaining that when Stone's letter arrived he had been in Atlantic City, where he had taken his five-year-old grandson on a little trip, just the two of them. "You should have seen us in Child's," Mr. Gaston wrote, "eating pancakes at eleven o'clock at night, mind you. Well, Jeff, be sure and give my regards to 'the boss' and don't eat too much junket."

A new cobweb was forming on the ceiling, and he watched its short wisp of tail move in the breeze that he could never feel on his face.

Stone lay on his cot. He knew that Shirley was sitting there and then was gone. He knew that in the ladies room next door the toilet was being flushed and that a woman was saying her room overlooked the alley and that Mr. Perry had his nerve asking four dollars a night for a room that never had any air because the window kept falling down unless she propped it up with a stick.

He knew that it was raining because, though the window with its view of blackness beneath the side porch, he could hear rain running down a downspout, and against the sound of the rain he could hear the louder than usual roar of the ocean.

When he went on duty, people came slamming into the taproom in raincoats, below which gleamed wet tanned shins and bare wet feet. They dashed the rain from their soaking hair and asked for a beer.

When he got back to his room he found Shirley there again, sitting gravely on his bed, in a clean white sweater to go with her clean blonde hair and smoothly tanned cheeks.

She moved a little so that Stone could lie down. Presently Stone heard her say, "She also needs a new snowsuit. My aunt gave her the old one but she's outgrown it already. She outgrew it last winter. It's only a Size Two-Toddler."

Stone nodded.

"She's going to be a human being, do you *realize* that, Jeff?" Shirley sighed, and in the sigh Stone heard both apprehension and ecstasy.

"Who?" he asked.

"My little girl. She's going to be a human being. I guess I'll get her a red one. I think red looks nice with blonde hair, don't you?"

"A red what?"

Shirley began to sob. "A red *snow-suit*, you lousy self-centered bastard," she said and hurried from the room.

Stone was called upstairs to the telephone and it was his mother saying he had gotten a letter from his draft board, and asking whether she should open it.

"Please," he said.

Over the long distance phone, he heard the sound of paper rustling. "It says—oh dear God—" His mother's voice faded.

"What does it say?" Stone asked.

"It says you're supposed to report for induction September 29."

"Okay," he said. "That's—exactly a month from today."

His mother quickly said that one of the girls in her bridge club knew an admiral who was sure there would be no war in the Pacific, and that Hitler had his hands full with Russia.

She said it very hopefully, and Stone smiled. He asked how things were at home, and the hope faded from his mother's voice, although her words were hopeful enough. She said his father was away on business.

"Jeff, honey, please don't be in a hurry to come home. After your job ends, maybe you could just stay on for a while and have some fun. Everything here is just fine, it really is. The boys are fine. In another two weeks they'll be going back to school."

Stone thanked her for calling about the letter from his draft board. He hung up, hearing what she had said about his brothers going back to school. It would seem strange, he thought, not to be going back to school, because for so many years that's what September had meant.

Stone knew that the boardwalk lights went off at two o'clock in the morning, and presently they were off.

Sitting on the beach, he looked back toward the hotel and saw Parker moving about in the dimly-lit lobby, going about his duties as night-clerk.

Stone got up and brushed the sand from his trousers. As he neared the boardwalk, he saw Parker standing on the front steps of the hotel, taking the air.

Parker came down the steps to meet him as he climbed up to the boardwalk from the sand. Parker yawned. He yawned again and said only a few days to go, and that he would be glad when his night clerk job ended because he found it hard to sleep in the daytime.

"Can you sit a few minutes?" Parker asked. "I'd like to talk to you." There was something different, Stone thought, about Parker's voice. It had a patronizing sound, the sound of confidence. Instead of rolling deep in his chest, it now crackled.

They sat in two rockers on the front porch of the hotel. Stone looked at the clean lines of Parker's profile, thinking how sharp they were. "I've been thinking about you," Parker said.

"About me?"

"Yes, I've been thinking about you a great deal. It's almost an obsession, Jeff. I can't deny it. And maybe by talking with you I can rid myself of it."

"What sort of obsession?"

"That you should have been so roughshod, so intemperate, so vainglorious, so self-indulgent, as to take a young girl and fornicate with her and then dump her."

"Do you mean Shirley?"

"Are there others?"

Stone could feel the hatred, could see it in Parker's death grip on each arm of the rocker. "A sad child whose father beat her and whose husband beat her—and you—when she was so vulnerable and susceptible."

"I'm sorry," Stone said.

"Are you truly sorry?"

"Yes, I'm *truly* sorry."

Parker stopped rocking. He glanced sharply in Stone's direction and then out into the blackness of the night that stretched from the unlit boardwalk over the black ocean toward Europe.

"Then there's hope," Parker said. "We've both watched you, wondering what's wrong with you. Shirley thinks it's because of the war. I think it is because of something deeper, that caused you to do what you did to Shirley." Parker's voice rose. "Which is it?"

Stone said nothing.

"The war? If it's the war, Jeff, you should come to terms with yourself. Are you afraid to die for your country, is that it?" Parker brought his fist down on the arm of the rocker. "Why not try Jesus?" he snapped.

"Ummm," Stone said.

Parker raised his right hand, index finger pointed upward. "Listen, this is no ordinary war, Hitler is no ordinary adversary. This is a war that threatens the very foundations of civilization, as it has been so carefully wrought over the centuries. Don't you understand that?"

"When you say dying for my country—what part of my country do you mean? Its trolley cars? Its clergy?"

"Nonsense! Its—rocks and rills and archives, its perpetuity."

Stone grunted.

"War," Parker said, "is inevitable, and the sooner we all realize it the better. No one should think for a moment that we're going to be able to stay *out* of it, Mr. Roosevelt's promises to the contrary notwithstanding."

Stone rocked, saying nothing.

"We certainly can't place too much faith in Russia. The

way Russia has been standing up to Hitler on the Eastern Front is a nice break for the Allies, of course . . ." Parker's voice had begun to reverberate. Now it dropped to a dramatic whisper and he had never seemed more unctuous. "But as the newspaper said this very morning, if we are to use every break that comes our way as a pleasant opportunity to snatch another forty winks, what will the harvest be?"

"God only knows," Stone said.

"Furthermore," Parker went on, "it's the Japs we've got to look out for, not just Hitler. Look how they're acting up, grabbing bases that don't belong to them and acting so arrogant. We've got to isolate *them* before they isolate *us*."

Parker lapsed in silence and began rocking, faster and faster. "I wish in a way," he said intensely, "the Japs *would* start something, so we can teach them a lesson."

Stone kept rocking, looking out over the ocean.

"Knowing that war is inevitable," Parker said, "what you probably should do is enlist instead of waiting to be drafted. With your college education you could probably get a commission. It may be quite a while yet before you hear from your draft board."

"Nope," Stone said.

"What do you mean?"

"I report September 29. My mother called me this evening."

Stone could hear the change in Parker's voice, and although Parker's intent was to make it merely curious, it was impossible not to hear the pleasure. "You mean your draft board has told you to report for induction September 29?"

"That's right," Stone said.

"How do you feel about it?"

"I knew it was coming," Stone said.

"Well . . ." Parker began to rock again, but in the way he was rocking there was something, Stone felt, that was somehow serene. "When we know something is inevitable, it's far better to face it sooner than later. I used that as the very theme of a sermon I preached at a funeral last winter. Well—so that by October you may be in army camp?"

"I suppose so," Stone said. "Or the navy."

"Well, I hope you'll be able to get off the weekend of October 18, because we're getting married that weekend and Shirley wants you to be there."

Parker was rocking so hard now that his feet left the floor.

"You and Shirley . . . are getting married?" Stone asked.

"Yes. October 19."

Stone got up from his chair and walked to the railing of the porch. The taproom was just below. He grasped the railing in both hands, looking down.

"Aren't you going to congratulate me?" Parker asked.

"Yes," Stone said. "I congratulate you."

"It has the ring of sincerity," Parker said. "I'm glad. Thank you."

"It's very sincere," Stone said. "I congratulate you."

"It wasn't possible," Parker said, "until she got over you. But now she is over you."

"That's good," Stone said. "I'm glad. Where will you live?"

"Somewhere in my neck of the woods to start out."

"In Virginia?"

"To start with, yes."

"Well, I hope you'll be very happy," Stone said. "She's a very wonderful girl."

Stone felt the thickness in his throat and heard it in his voice. He turned away again, and then said goodnight and went down to his room.

✳ twenty-six

One of the very worst things in the world, Stone thought, would be to be a small animal moving about from day to day and then to see on the ground the shadow of vast wings, a shadow swiftly moving, and then to be lifted from the ground in the claws of an eagle and borne aloft, squealing and whimpering. The habitat of eagles would be one of vast cathedral silence.

Turning off the light, he lay on his cot and began to whistle various instrumental choruses from Count Basie's recording of *Topsy*.

It was a very loud clear whistle, with trilling and warbling effects, as if the person whistling considered himself a very accomplished whistler and moreover made it plain that the person had memorized it all, note for note.

All the next day he whistled trumpet and tenor saxophone choruses from various Basie recordings. Buddy told him that he sure could whistle.

That night, when Mr. Perry came down to check the cash, he and Buddy got into a discussion of toothpastes. Mr. Perry told Stone and Buddy the brand of toothpaste he used and asked them what they thought of it.

"I use it because none of your gol-dairned dentists recommend it," Mr. Perry said.

"Why is that, sir?" Buddy asked.

"Well, any dentist that wants to keep cavities out of your teeth is a plain dairned fool or liar or both," Mr. Perry said. "If people stopped having cavities, all your dentists would starve to death. So when I heard about a toothpaste that dentists recommend I know very well it's going to shoot my teeth full of holes, eating away the porcelain and what-not."

Mr. Perry bared his teeth, taking a forefinger and drawing his upper lip back to reveal his gums. "Look how nice my teeth are for a man my age," he said. "Not to brag, but I think I have dairned nice teeth for my age, Jeff, how about it?"

Stone said yes, that he certainly seemed to.

"Hey, man!" William called.

Stone answered, and William said he was just back from Philadelphia, where his mother was resting comfortably after being struck by an Austin. William said that in his opinion if you had to be struck by anything it was better to be struck by a midget car like an Austin, and his mother agreed, although his brother felt that the driver of the Austin had struck their mother deliberately because of her race.

On the hard damp sand, Stone ran at top speed as far as he could, and when he was exhausted and his head was pounding, he flopped into the ocean.

When he came out, he was followed by a gangling Irish setter puppy. He turned suddenly, and the puppy drew up short and sat on its haunches, looking at him, tongue lolling.

Confronting the puppy, Stone raised his right hand and pointed his index finger to the sky. "And lo!" he bellowed at the puppy. "And Jesus went into the valley of shadows and a shadow said unto Jesus, 'Master wherefore is my substance?' And Jesus replied unto him, 'The answer resideth in the question, get thee hence.' "

Stone started off and then looked back. The puppy was still sitting in a loose-jointed, awkward way. "Why not try Jesus?" Stone snapped over his shoulder.

Nearing the hotel, he saw Shirley coming down the front steps, headed for the mailbox with letters in her hand.

As she returned, he grinned up at her from the sand.

"Oh, *there* you are," she said.

"Yes, *here* I am. Hey, Shirl . . ."

"What?"

Stone grinned.

"What's *wrong* with you?" she demanded.

"And lo!" Stone said. "I say unto you—fuck you!"

She started down at him. "What's *wrong* with you?"

"And lo!" Stone said. "I say unto you, I hope you will be happy, all the days of your life, even unto death. Apocrypha."

Her face was twisted and he was not sure whether it was with anger or concern.

"And I say unto you," he said, grinning, "when you are nailed to the cross with purple light bulbs, remember that but for the grace of God it might be the A. & P. So be it."

Stone turned and walked slowly down to the ocean. He moved through the shallows and dived through a wave. When he turned and looked back, she had gone into the hotel.

He kept riding waves until he saw her come out of the hotel, move down the steps and move to the edge of the boardwalk, waving and beckoning. Deliberately he walked across the sand until he could hear her. "*Telephone* . . ." she was calling. "You can't come through the lobby like that. Go around back, up through the bathhouse entrance."

It was his mother, and this time she was sobbing. She told him that his father had left home that morning, with two suitcases. Stone told her he would be home the next evening.

Retracing his steps down through the bathhouse, he went out into the ocean again, letting the waves toy with his body, springing lightly from the sand and letting himself be borne with the swells. He looked up at a cloud, telling himself that it wasn't really a cloud but the face of God. Squinting, he asked aloud, "What in the hell are you trying to *pull,* what the hell's *happened* to you?"

Shirley's mother and daughter had arrived to take Shirley back to Pennsylvania, and Parker would go along to meet the rest of Shirley's huge family.

"That's nice," Stone said.

Shirley glared at him.

"I'm serious," he said. "I think that's nice."

Shirley asked if she could bring her child down to his room and Stone said no.

"Are you serious?" she demanded. "She won't hurt anything. She's good. How could she mess up a pigpen like this anyway. Oh, you bastard . . ."

Stone heard Shirley running along the corridor.

"Well, only one more day," Buddy said and Stone said, "Yeah."

Buddy said: "Shirley asked me to tell you there's going to be a talent show for kids and her kid's going to be in it. She wants you to come up and watch, I think—except she told me to tell you she didn't give a damn whether you came up and watched or not."

"Okay," Stone said.

"She said her kid was going to do a toe-dance," Buddy said. "And anyway, we've both got to be here and help out, my uncle says. At first they were going to have it upstairs in the Chinese Checkers room but my uncle thought they'd mess it up, so it's going to be here, in the bar."

"Okay," Stone said.

"Hey, Stoney, are you okay?"

"Hell, yes," Stone said. "I'm fine. How are you, Buddy?"

Buddy grinned. "Okay, I guess."

"Did you ever get laid?"

Buddy shook his head sheepishly. "Nope. I have to be honest."

"Well, don't worry," Stone said. "It's over-rated anyway."

Buddy laughed and said that was not what he had heard.

In the Children's Talent Contest, there were ten entries—ten children, lifted in turn up to the bar by Buddy and Stone.

After a while Stone let Buddy do all the work. He retreated into the storeroom and sat on the beer cases, not looking through the open doorway, not seeing the children jitterbugging but hearing the juke box music to which they jitterbugged, and then hearing the female child who sang a folk song in a childish voice, followed by loud applause.

Mr. Perry then made a speech, saying how glad he was that all the children were there and how talented they all were and how he wished his aging pelvis would permit him to "do the jitterbug," whereupon several of the mothers shouted, "Oh go on, do it" and from the laughter and applause Stone judged that Mr. Perry had done it. Mr. Perry then asked Stone peevishly what he was doing back in the storeroom and to come out and serve free cokes to all ten children and if their mothers wanted to buy beer they could, at no advance in prices, whereupon the mothers laughed weakly.

Stone uncapped ten cokes, of which six were quickly spilled. He did not see Shirley and judged that none of the ten children was hers. He looked again to make sure she was not there, reaching then for a rag to help wipe brown droplets and streaks from clip-on bowties and short skirts airborne with starch. Mr. Perry then directed Stone to supply six additional cokes to replace the six that were spilled, whereupon a boy with a widow's peak bit the wrist of a girl with bangs and she spilled her coke and the boy's mother said he didn't mean it, and the boy said he did mean it, he really *meant* it. Stone replaced the six replacement cokes on a table, causing an accelerated snake dance in the course of which three more cokes were overturned and Mr. Perry said, "No more now, children, no more now," muttering, "I own this place lock, stock and barrel, I've never seen such God-damn children in all my life."

When it was over, Stone went back to his room and lay on his cot. Presently he heard footsteps along the corridor, running and then abruptly stopping. The screen door was shoved open and she looked in.

"B-b-b-but," she said.

✳ twenty-seven

Stone looked at her steadily.

"But why do you live d-d-d-down *here?*" she asked with concern.

Stone said just because he did, and she stood clinging to the edge of the screen door, opening it and closing it, hanging on it.

Stone had the impression that he was looking at a painting. From a short plaid skirt, her legs dangled delicately, daintily. She was fragile of knee, and of purest brow serene.

He asked if she was lost and she said yes, she thought so. She edged closer to the cot, still warily keeping one hand on the screen door.

She was dancing a ballet with the door, rising now and

then on one toe. Her black shoes glittered and her eyes were enormous, with gorgeous thick lashes that struck him from across the room each time she swept them down over her eyes. He had an impression of grey, yet there was no grey in her lashes, nor in her pure blonde, haphazardly curling hair. He concluded that the grey must be in her eyes, which were not quite blue.

He asked her to come closer, and she shook her head, smiling. "You might hurt me," she said.

Stone smiled and shook his head.

She pointed to the hole in the wall, asking why it was there.

Stone said so he could talk to the man next door.

"Will the man next door hurt me?" she asked.

Stone said no.

"I want to s-s-s-s . . ."

"What?" Stone asked quietly.

She smiled. "I want to s-s-s-*see* him."

Stone said there was no way, because of the wall and that all she could do was to talk to him through the hole.

"Why?" she asked.

Stone said, "Just because."

She laughed uncertainly. Her tiny fingernails were lined up along the edge of the screen door, each with the chipped remains of pink polish.

Stone sat up in bed, and at the sudden movement she backed quickly into the corridor, closing the screen door but still peering in, her blonde hair screened now by the filthy dusty mesh. "Lie down again," she said.

Stone obeyed.

The door opened again and she came in, telling him she had a bear named Doolittle.

Stone said that was a nice name.

"I love birds, they're very nice, they sing," she said, **and** she sang.

"Why is *that* there?" she asked, pointing to his raincoat, which hung over the window that looked out upon the underside of the porch.

Stone said just because it was.

"Take it off," she said.

Stone removed the raincoat.

In the distance, he could hear Shirley calling, "Laurie . . ."

"That's my m-m-m-m-mommy calling me," she said. Releasing the screen door, she put her hands on her hips and shouted, "What?" Grabbing fast to the door again, she laughed. "She wants me," she explained to Stone.

Her attention returned to the window, which he had always thought of as a window and called a window in his mind, but which, he knew was nothing but an oblong opening over which filthy screening had been tacked, only that and the darkness beyond.

She was looking gravely into the darkness beyond the screen. "B-b-b-but . . ." she said, turning as Shirley appeared.

"How did you get down here?" Shirley asked, looking at Stone.

"I just comed," the child said.

Shirley bent to kiss the top of her head. "Laurie," she said, "this is Mr. Stone."

Smiling, Laurie grabbed the edge of the screen door and held tight.

"Say goodbye to Mr. Stone."

"Goodbye, Laurie," Stone said. He looked at Shirley. Shirley was looking at the child.

Laurie smiled back over her shoulder.

Stone heard them walking along the corridor. He heard the child's voice saying, "He didn't hurt me."

Because it was the last day and almost everybody was

gone, Mr. Perry said to close the taproom at three in the afternoon. Since the taproom never opened until noon, that meant it would only be open three hours, which Buddy said hardly would be worth it. Stone agreed but didn't care.

Since it was the last day, Buddy suggested that they should not divide the shift but work the whole three hours together, just for old time's sake.

There was very little business, and Buddy talked at some length of how mature he had grown from working in the taproom and seeing what people were really like.

He said he wondered what had happened to Charlie. "I wonder what happens to a guy like that," he said. Stone said he didn't know, but he had been thinking at that same moment of Charlie, of how Charlie had coached him to say, "We're waitin' for the bread man, I don't know what's keepin' that bastard," when people asked for sandwiches.

Mr. Perry came down at ten minutes of three. Taking what little money there was from the cash register, he asked Buddy when he was leaving, and Buddy said in an hour or so.

"Well, don't forget to give my love to your mother and father and all," Mr. Perry said.

He asked Stone when he was leaving, and Stone said he wasn't sure but pretty soon.

Mr. Perry frowned. "Well, I'll expect you to be out no later than six o'clock," he said. "The season's over. Everybody has to clear out."

Stone nodded.

"Are you all packed?" Mr. Perry asked.

Stone said he didn't have much to pack but that it was packed.

"Are you taking the bus?"

Stone said he was.

"Well, it's been nice having you and everything," Mr.

Perry said. "And you've been good at your work and all. I guess I owe you an apology in a way, for thinking you might have been the one taking the money. But you probably remember of course the time I gave you Noxzema for your sunburn."

Stone said that he did.

"Well then," Mr. Perry said.

Stone thanked him again for the Noxzema.

"Okay then," Mr. Perry said, and, putting the cash into his blue denim sack, he stomped out.

Stone went to his room and lay on the cot, looking at the ceiling. The new cobweb had grown larger and blacker and was floating short distances in the breeze that always came from nowhere.

When Shirley came down, she said that Parker, after being up all night, had not slept that morning and was now taking a little nap before they all left. She said she and her mother and child were going to walk up the boardwalk, and although she knew he would say no, she had come down anyway to ask him if he wanted to go along.

Stone said yes.

"What time does your bus leave?" she asked.

"Five-thirty," he said.

They walked up the boardwalk, and the sharp September light dazzled his eyes.

Shirley's mother was short and thick and wore glasses with lenses so fat that they gave her huge blurred eyes. She wondered if she was making a mistake in buying salt water taffy to take home to Shirley's Aunt Beatrice, whose teeth were mostly false. She concluded that it would be possible for Aunt Beatrice to let the salt water taffy melt gradually in her mouth and Shirley concurred.

"You should have brought a sweater for that child," Shirley's mother said. "The air's chilly. This is September."

Stone felt a hand slip into his own. He looked down and she looked up at him. "Hi, Laurie," he said.

"Shall I get it in here?" Shirley's mother asked.

"Yes, mother," Shirley said. "It's the only place open."

When her mother went into the salt water taffy store, Shirley said, "She asks me everything. She can't ever make a decision for herself. Doesn't everything look strange—so empty. Everybody gone."

The child ran off and Shirley ran to retrieve her. Stone saw them down the boardwalk together. He watched them return. The child's hand was in Shirley's. They wore mother and daughter dresses of light blue and they had mother and daughter blonde hair, lit by the September sun.

Stone looked at them and then away from them, turning toward the blue and white September ocean. Then he looked at them again and, looking away, felt dizzy, the way he had felt when he noticed the sweep of the child's eyelashes.

"I guess she'll just have to gum it," Shirley's mother said with the salt water taffy box under her arm.

"Doolittle hurt his leg," the child said. "But it's all b-b-b-better now." She took Stone's hand again. Her lips were parted. They were tiny, smooth, damp, fragile lips and it gave him pleasure to know that they were not at all like a rosebud.

The child ran ahead, turning to smile back at Stone.

Stone looked at her and what he felt for the child flew from child to mother, and from mother to child, and the complete appeal of one became the appeal of the other.

"It's so hard to get her to go near anybody," Shirley's mother said. "You've made a hit with her. She doesn't like Bob much, I can tell you that."

"She will in time," Shirley said.

The sky was clear ice blue, fed from a mountain stream, and bluer still in the patches surrounded by the deeply textured white clouds. Among the clouds there was a rounded pool of rich pale blue and Stone, looking up, wanted to bend and drink from it.

"She wants to see your room again, Jeff," Shirley said. "She's fascinated by it."

"But not too long," Shirley's mother said. "We have to wake Bob up and leave."

Stone sat on the cot while the child stood next to the orange crate, patting it and smiling at him.

"But-but-but . . ."

"You see how she stutters, so often it's B's," Shirley said. "But I'm sure she'll get over it and my mother thinks so too."

Stone picked up the child and kissed the pale smoothness of her brow, holding her for a moment very close, overcome with a need to protect her fragility, to keep her delicate knees from hurt, to shield her from the pain that would come because she stuttered, to protect her, and thereby to protect himself.

Carefully he let her down to the floor again and kissed the top of her head.

Shirley's eyes were glistening. "I'll see you again, won't I, Jeff? Some day? Will you come to the wedding?"

Stone shook his head. "I don't think so." Looking steadily into her eyes, he muttered, "Whose wedding?"

"Ours?" Shirley said.

The child was looking at the dirty screen that framed the darkness. "What's in there?"

Stone said nothing was in there.

"Is it b-b-b-bad things in there?"

Stone said no.

The child continued to stare with fascination at the screen and the darkness beyond, then looked first at Shirley and then at Stone.

God. He picked Laurie up again, clasping her tight with his left arm behind her knees, and with his right arm he picked up Shirley, holding them high, feeling the strength in his arms, feeling exultation and feeling the power to move, walk, stride, carry, to burst through the walls of gloom, the walls of his tiny world, to run out into the sunlight, to drink from the sky.

The child struggled at first and then grew still, and for long moments, as he continued to hold them aloft, they both seemed to be waiting in silence, two figures in a tableau, a mother and child, one in each arm.

Stooping, he eased them to the floor. "Goodbye, Laurie," he said.

"Jeff . . ." Shirley said. "Will you kiss me goodbye? *Please?*"

Stone kissed her and she let her body fall against him, clinging, not letting go. "I'll always love you, Jeff," she whispered. "All the rest of my life."

"Don't, Shirl," he said. He was thinking of the afternoon they had walked up the beach and she had grabbed a handful of sand and thrown it into the air, letting it drift with the wind. "I'm not worth it. I'm a stupid dumb bastard. I love you very much."

They both heard the footsteps and then the sound of Parker's mighty voice, rolling and reverberating along the darkened corridor. "Coming, Shirley? Come on, let's go. Come on, Laurie, Grandmom is waiting."

Shirley dabbed at her eyes and picked up the child. "Good luck, Jeff," she said, and was gone. Their footsteps faded.

Stone stood alone in his room, seeing and feeling its emptiness, and hearing its silence. *Whaddya think,* he asked Christ, and Christ replied, *I think you're a self-centered little bastard who likes to live in small rooms.* Picking up the orange crate, Stone smashed it against the huge white pillar and let the splintered wood lay where it fell.

Wearing his seersucker jacket and carrying a small suitcase, Stone walked along the back streets toward the bus depot. As he walked, he whistled clear loud notes, telling himself there was no essential difference between feeling and not feeling, loving and not loving, that to a machine it was all the same because no course was better or worse than its opposite. When his lips began to tremble and his throat grew tight, he stopped whistling and walked on through the pale sunlight of the September late afternoon.